A BEST-SELLING SERIES IN CHINA
盗墓筆記

THE GRAVE ROBBERS' CHRONICLES

VOL 3

Bronze Tree of Death

BY XU LEI

TRANSLATED BY KATHY MOK

The Grave Robbers' Chronicles: Volume 3
Bronze Tree of Death
By Xu Lei
Translated by Kathy Mok

Edited by Janet Brown and Michelle Wong
Illustrated by Vladimir Verano

ThingsAsian Press
San Francisco, California USA
www.thingsasianpress.com
Printed in China

ISBN-13: 978-1-934159-33-0
ISBN-10: 1-934159-33-6

TABLE OF CONTENTS

CHAPTER ONE

REUNION WITH A JAILBIRD

"The fish is at my place."

What fish? Could this be the third Bronze Fish with Snake Brows?

The carving in the undersea tomb showed three of these fish all connected, head to tail. I had two of them but there ought to be one more. Did this sentence mean someone else had the third fish?

I scrolled through the notice once more and saw it had been posted two years ago. There was no contact information for the person who had put it on the Internet, nor could I find any other links to the post. Whoever had put this online had a photo of Uncle Three's group—and knew about the fish. Who could this be?

When the storm cleared, we were more than ready to leave the island, but first we went to the hospital to check on Ning. She was gone, the doctor told us, taken away by a group of foreigners a few days before.

"God damn it," Fats grumbled, "she got away again."

"It's a good thing. What were we going to do with her? We couldn't torture her to make her tell us who she worked for or what she knew about the tomb," I said. "Now she's the foreigners' problem, not ours. She's never been anything but a big pain in the ass—I'm glad she's gone."

Nevertheless, it was plain that when the company she had worked for asked us to find their missing boat, they had more at stake than one lost vessel. What had they really been searching for? Did my uncle know? Had he been working with them? Where was he now? Would the answers to these questions ever emerge from the South China Sea? Or did they lie elsewhere, in a place I had not yet explored?

I said goodbye to Qilin and Fats and was back home in Hangzhou within four hours. It was amazing how smoothly things went once I was no longer under the influence of my Uncle Three in any way. It was a relief to bid farewell to the tombs and zombies and corpses; I was ready to resume my real life once more.

After sleeping in my own bed for more than twenty-four hours—the first real slumber I'd had in months—I called my shop assistant and found everything was as it should be in the business side of my life. Then I called my family to find out if any of them had heard from my uncle—he was still missing. Finally I called his shop and asked one of his employees, "Has Third Master Wu come by?"

The clerk hesitated and said, "No but a strange man came in. He said he was your brother and insisted that we tell him where you were. I have no idea where he came from but judging by his manners, he didn't look like someone from a good family, so I sent him packing. But he left you his phone number. Would you like to have it?"

What the hell—I had many acquaintances, but not many who would go to Uncle Three to look for me. I thought for a moment and asked, "How old was this guy?"

"I can't be sure, probably about your age, but he looked in worse shape than you ever have. Flattop hairstyle, small eyes. Wore glasses and an earring. Inarticulate."

"Inarticulate?" I repeated. "Did he have a speech impediment?"

"Right, right, right. He stuttered twelve times before he could finish a sentence."

"Got it, thanks." I quickly wrote down the phone number and made a call. A familiar voice on the other end stammered, "Who—who—who is it?"

I laughed. "Fuck you, don't you know who I am?"

He was silent for a moment and then said, "Three—three—three years since I last heard your voice. Of course I didn't recognize it. "

"What the hell? I didn't hear from you either," I protested, "I thought you were dead."

It was Lao Yang. I'd stopped using his real name long ago. We grew up like brothers; we did everything together. At one point we even looked alike. His family was poor and after he graduated from college, he couldn't find a job, so he came to work for me at my shop.

His stutter made his speech slow but Lao Yang could charm anyone with his words, once he got them out. We worked well together and the shop made money—good times.

Unfortunately, Lao Yang made a big mistake: he went off with one of his cousins to rob graves over in the Qinling Mountains and got caught. The cousin was sentenced to life, but Lao Yang used his gift of gab to portray himself as a promising young man who'd been led astray and he received only three years in prison.

I tried to visit him when he first went in, but he was humiliated; he refused to see me and we lost contact. I only heard his name once in three years, when that strange old man came to my shop with the map to the cavern of the blood zombies. I had no idea my old buddy had finally gotten out of jail.

I felt partly responsible for his running off to become a grave robber. From the time we were little, I bragged to him about my cool grave-robbing grandfather and the treasures he had looted. Probably that planted the seed that had sent him off with his cousin to find what they could in the mountain tombs.

He always was more daring than I was. When we were kids, I was the one with the ideas but he put them into practice—and always got in trouble as a result. Still I never thought he'd turn to grave robbing—or that I would either.

We had a lot to talk about, with three years to catch up on, and once we got started we couldn't shut up.

"You're not doing anything tonight, right? I'll take you to dinner," I suggested.

"That—that's not a bad idea. I haven't had a good meal in three years. I'll be happy to let you buy me one."

I was so eager to see Lao Yang that I got to the restaurant early and ordered all of his favorite dishes. When he showed up, we didn't chat too much at first but in no time we drank half a bottle of wine. It wasn't until we'd emptied every plate on the table and turned them upside down that we realized we were having trouble talking to each other now that we were face-to-face.

I was more than a little drunk and, belching loudly, I asked, "Tell me honestly. What the hell did you loot that caused your cousin to get a life sentence?"

Once I asked him that, I regretted it. If I upset him, it might not be easy to resume our old friendship. But my question made him puff up with pride. “The stuff we got—you’ll never believe what I tell you.”

His condescension really pissed me off. “I’m not the college kid you left three years ago. I know a thing or two about tomb treasures. Whatever dynasty your discovery came from, be it Tang, Song, Yuan, Ming, or Qing—as long as you can describe it, I can tell you what it is and its age too.”

Lao Yang looked at me and smiled. “Look—look at you with your Tang, Song, Yuan, Ming, and Qing bullshit!” Then he dipped his chopsticks into his wine and drew a weird shape on the table. “Have—have you ever seen this before?”

I was drunk, my vision was blurry, and I couldn’t quite make out whether he’d drawn a tree or some sort of statue. “After three years behind bars, your drawing skills haven’t improved at all. What is this?”

Lao Yang replied, “You—you—you look again.”

I still couldn’t tell what he was driving at. “How the devil could anyone tell what you drew? You meant to draw some forklike patterns, right, but they look like tree branches instead. This drawing is so bad, I can’t tell what this is meant to be.”

Lao Yang smiled, lowered his voice, and said to me in a mysterious tone, “You—you are brilliant. These are just what you said they are—tree branches, bronze tree branches as thick as your wrist.”

Ah, so this guy looted some bronze. That was really pushing it. Three years was no time at all to serve for that crime. I asked, “So you couldn’t go for the small stuff—you had to go big-time. Were you that eager to go to prison?”

He patted my shoulder. “You don’t understand. That place was different from anything you could imagine. It’s a long story.”

I stared at his drawing and remembered the bronze forest dug up not long ago at Sanxingdui. This looked a lot like photos I'd seen of those trees.

Sanxingdui was in the land of ancient Shu, which is now Sichuan. Nothing from there could be sold on the antique market—it was far too ancient and far too rare, truly priceless. If Lao Yang had found something like that, it was hard to say if he had been lucky or cursed.

"Tell me all about this," I said. He took a huge gulp of wine and began his story.

He and his cousin had been in the Qinling Mountains for more than ten days. They had discovered nothing other than an unending forest that stretched before them, and they had almost run out of food and ammunition.

Neither of the men had any idea of how to rob a grave; all they had going for them was enthusiasm. At this point, the cousin was ready to give up and only Lao Yang's determination kept the expedition on track.

One day, they trekked to a mountain valley which contained a vast forest of gigantic banyan trees, so huge that ten men with outstretched arms would be unable to encircle any of them. The forest was so thick that it blocked out all sunlight, and the tree roots obscured the forest floor, like snakes curled up together in a tangled coil.

"These are too thick to dig through—or even walk through. Let's turn around," Lao Yang said as they struggled to walk through the snarls of roots. But now the cousin was the one who was reluctant to go back and he led the way deeper into the forest.

They could hear owls calling, and then darkness fell. They turned on their flashlights and slowed their steps, but even so the cousin tripped and nearly fell. Lao Yang quickly went over to help him gain his balance and found something wrapped in the banyan tree roots beneath their feet.

They chopped at the spot with their hatchets, pointed their flashlights at the object, and discovered a stone figure of a man, embossed with a beautiful design and covered with moss. Rummaging about where they found the figure, they uncovered many large cobblestones buried beneath the leaf-covered forest floor.

"It's a trail," the cousin said, "and this statue was probably the guardian of the road. Perhaps it's a path to an imperial tomb. Remember how an old man in the last town said there were noblemen from the Western Jin dynasty buried up in these valleys?"

He and his cousin decided to follow the trail. If there was an ancient tomb nearby, there would certainly be traces of it left behind.

After a few hours, they entered the heart of the woodland. More moss-covered stone figures lay on both sides of the pathway. Certain they were on the right track, the men hurried even faster, but the farther they went the thicker grew the banyan roots, as if the trees wanted no strangers in their midst.

They continued to walk until late at night when they were both exhausted. Moonlight began to gleam through the thick forest and Lao Yang was sure that the stone path had come to an end. They climbed over a jumbled pile of rocks, hacked through the last of the banyan roots, and emerged from the forest.

Suddenly a huge crater appeared in the moonlight, as big as a football field, like a gigantic grave surrounded by the forest. In the slope of this pit a staircase was carved, with about a hundred steps that led down into the depths of the crater.

Lao Yang's cousin said, "This place must have been part of a sacrificial rite; it looks like an altar. Why don't we go down, take a look, and see if there are any burial objects lying around?"

The moon was clear and white but the ground in front of the two men was covered in darkness. They beamed their flashlights into the night to keep from being tripped by the snakelike roots and cautiously followed the stone steps down to the bottom of the pit.

Its four sides were completely hidden by the banyan trees that encircled it. Had they not followed the ancient trail, they would never have discovered it even if they'd walked nearby. The cobblestones within the pit were in segments like pieces of a jigsaw puzzle, with a large number of roots extruding from the stones and extending into the sides. At the center of the pit was a well encircled by stones in the middle of what they were sure was a sacrificial altar. At the bottom of the well was no water, only grass, so they rappelled to the bottom, shovels in hand, and began to dig.

After an hour of digging they had found nothing of value. Cinders were mixed in the dirt they excavated along with bits of pottery and jade, shards of sacrificial offerings burned for the dead. The well had been used for this purpose more than once, they realized.

Lao Yang's mind began to whirl with excitement. Gorgeous pieces of pottery and jade were often part of burial ceremonies. If they could find one or two unbroken vessels, they would never have to work again.

But his elation was soon dampened by the reality of their

discoveries. They uncovered a pile of fragments but nothing that wasn't broken. "All of this work and nothing valuable, what a fucking waste of time," he mumbled under his breath.

"We need to stop," his cousin responded. "If we dig any further, the well may collapse and bury us alive. If we've gone this far and found nothing, it's almost certain that there's no treasure here. Tough luck but that's the chance a grave robber has to take."

Lao Yang paid no attention and continued to dig, even though his cousin went back to the surface, leaving him alone in the well. After two hours of hard work, he was almost ready to give up when he heard a clanging sound. His shovel had struck metal.

His cousin leaped back down when he heard the noise, and he and Lao Yang peered into the hole. Something that glowed dark brownish green jutted from the middle of the well. Shouting and laughing, the two men began to paw the dirt away from the object with their bare hands. As they uncovered the top of it, they saw it was a branch of a tree, made completely from bronze.

Neither of them had ever seen anything like this before and they knew it had to be immensely valuable. Furiously, they dug to reach its base but it was hidden far below the earth. They tried with all of their strength to pull it up but it was impossible to move. Using their shovels, they dug for another hour but failed to reach the base of that one branch.

"This is weird," Lao Yang observed. "I've worked with antiques for a long time and have rarely seen anything made from bronze that is over nine feet long, but this thing, judging by how far we've dug, has to be much, much longer than that. What in the hell have we found here?"

They had come too far for safety—the tunnel they had dug was sure to collapse at any moment, but neither of the men wanted to give up without bringing their discovery with them. Lao Yang's cousin cursed; walking three feet away from the branch, he pushed his shovel into the ground at a slanted angle. He threaded a pipe on the handle and pounded it into the soil. It went down about thirty feet and then no further.

As Lao Yang told me this part of his story, his expression twisted as he spoke. He took a long drag on his cigarette. "According to our calculations, the total length of that branch was at least thirty feet. It would have been impossible for us to bring it out of that well, assuming we could even dig it free."

I stared at him without speaking. He had to be exaggerating, if not lying. The largest piece of cast bronze ever found in China was a tripod unearthed in Henan and that was only about three feet tall. Even that would have taken the combined efforts of two to three hundred people all working at the same time to cast during that period of history. To make an object as huge as the one Lao Yang described would have employed over ten thousand workers, an incredible project that completely boggled my mind.

But feeling it would be rude to express my doubts, I asked, "Then what happened? Did you keep on digging?"

"No," he replied, "I wanted to but my cousin pointed out that this thing might be sacred. Maybe it had been buried deep underground; certainly it was impossible to dig up. I gave up but I can't forget about it. This is something that could shock the entire world if it were excavated; I'd love to be the man who brought it to light."

1. REUNION WITH A JAILBIRD

"If you came back empty-handed, why were you arrested and put in prison?"

"It was my cousin's fault," he said. "We found a few other pits and dug up some unbroken pots, but there was nothing special. When we got back, we started to look for a place to unload our loot. But that bronze branch had made my cousin crazy; he talked about it to everyone he met. When we finally found an antique shop that would do business with us, my cousin started telling the people there his story and they called the police. I was lucky, the cop who arrested me was an old friend and he got me three years for being an unwitting dupe. My cousin would have gotten off with four or five years but he went nuts and confessed to every grave-robbing expedition he had ever been told about. He ended up with a life sentence and was lucky not to have been executed."

"You're too fucking much," I told Lao Yang. "How could you live so long and learn so little? Never ever get rid of loot in the area where you found it, you moron. What happened to you is retribution pure and simple—you were stupid and you paid for it."

Lao Yang smiled. "But look. I didn't come away with nothing—look at this." He pointed toward his earring.

CHAPTER TWO

THE HEXAGONAL BELL

I leaned closer to take a look, grabbed his earlobe, and held it right in front of me so I could examine what was there. The earring was boxy and about the size of my thumb. It could easily be mistaken for a cheap, two-for-one-yuan earring sold at a roadside stall. But it was actually a hexagonal bell, with a size and color almost identical to the ones I saw in the cavern of the blood zombies and in the undersea tomb. The only difference was this one was slightly smaller, with patterns on it that were unlike ones on the others I had seen.

I sobered up immediately. Still clutching Lao Yang's ear, I asked, "Where the hell did you find this?"

He whimpered from the pain of my grip. "God damn it, you've had too much to drink. Let go of my ear or I'll beat you to a pulp."

"Sorry, you're right. I guess I'm drunk," I apologized, as I released him.

"Holy shit," Lao Yang grimaced, rubbing his ear. "You don't have to get so carried away just because I've shown you something good. My ear will never be the same; you've disfigured it forever."

"Stop kidding around and tell me right now. Where did

you find this bell?"

"You've never seen anything like it, have you? I knew you'd die of jealousy when I showed you. I got this from a zombie's body in a burial pit. How about that? Look—it's first-rate bronze, not like the crap you see in this city."

"What zombie? Didn't you say you only dug up some pots and pans? Now there's a zombie involved here?"

Thinking I spoke out of envy, Lao Yang became arrogant. "The zombie was wrapped in a cocoon with rattan ropes. I found it when I was digging up the pit, probably a high-status human sacrifice. It was wearing this thing on its ear and I liked the way it looked so I took it. Why are you acting so nervous? What do you know about this earring anyway? Is it worth something?"

My mind raced in a welter of confusion; I couldn't keep track of all the thoughts that popped up at the same time. I frowned. Where was this place? Why would this kind of bell turn up there? Could that pit Lao Yang found be linked in some way to the cavern of the blood zombies and the undersea tomb?

"What's wrong?" Lao Yang asked. "Why do you look so worried? We're buddies, if you like the damned earring so much, I'll give it to you."

"I won't hide the truth from you. I've seen your earring before. I don't know what it's meant for or where it came from but I know it's very special and may be quite important. Listen..."

I quickly told him what happened in the cavern of the blood zombies and in the undersea tomb, focusing mainly on the bells. His face turned as white and damp as a fish's belly; he said nothing.

When he recovered his equilibrium, he sighed. "Fuck me. I thought three years in prison would be enough for me to brag about for a lifetime. But that's nothing compared to your experiences. You'd be executed by a firing squad if you were caught for the stuff you've done."

"What's to envy? If I knew ahead of time that grave robbing was such a pain in the ass, I wouldn't have gone to those places even if you stuck a knife in my ribs and told me to go or die." I pointed to his ear and said, "But your bell is pretty weird. This type of bell is dangerous—once it rings, it poisons people's minds and hypnotizes them. How come you can wear it without suffering its effects?"

"It's not as scary as you think. Here, I'll take it off so you can have a better look." He handed me the earring.

I put it directly under the light, smelled it, and immediately knew how Lao Yang could wear it without falling under its spell. Rosin had been poured inside to keep the bell from making a sound. I flipped it over and examined it carefully. The more I looked, the more I knew it had to be related to the ones in the undersea tomb and in the cavern of carcasses.

Lao Yang was sure that I liked his earring since I scrutinized it so thoroughly. He put it back on and said, "If you think it's something you'd want, there are so many in that place. It's full of undiscovered, untouched zombies. I left my mark there. We can go back and take a look." He looked around, lowered his voice, and said, "To tell you the truth, I'm not doing so well. I'm planning to go back in the next few days and try my luck at another round. We could go together."

"No way. I don't want to end up in prison. Forget about it

and settle into the life of an honest man."

Lao Yang leaned over and whispered, "You—you can't say that. Think about it. You have your family backing you up. You can do whatever you want. I have wasted three years of my life, and I have nothing. I have to use my brain to make something of myself; I can't just sit around wasting my time."

He didn't look like he was kidding. I cursed, "Dream on, damn it. Three years in prison and you didn't learn a thing from your sentence. If you're caught again, you'll probably be executed on the spot."

"If I'm really that unlucky, then that's the way it's going to be," Lao Yang said with a tinge of resentment. "I don't have a choice. I have to do this; I've thought about it already. First I'll stay in Hangzhou for a while, then I'll go back to the Qinling Mountains. I came to you because I need help financing this. I hope you'll come with me, brother."

I snapped back, "What do you mean you don't have a choice? You just don't have money. How much do you need? I'll give it to you with a 5 percent discount on the fixed-rate interest the Bank of China is charging."

"It's not like I don't know what your assets are. I know you can easily take out tens of thousands. But do you have more than that? Really, why pretend to be rich when I know you aren't?"

"You're turning up your nose at tens of thousands of yuan. What the hell do you want with more money than that? Did you spot a star that you think you could buy for your own? You've just been fed—and quite well at my expense. Now I'm offering you a tidy sum. But you asshole, you just got out of prison and you're already on your way back into a cell. Grow up, damn it."

"Fuck you," Lao Yang yelled, and the whole restaurant turned to listen. "My business has nothing to do with you. If you don't want to join me, don't, but don't come here and lecture me either. Just forget it. This is a brotherly reunion. If you don't want to help, it's okay. Let's not talk anymore about things that spoil our pleasure this evening." He poured me another glass of wine.

He was looking down his nose at me while I was swimming in alcohol—not a good idea. I became even more pissed off. "I told you already, Lao Yang, don't condescend to me. I have a little more cash than you know about that I've gathered over the past few years. Why don't you honestly tell me how much you need? I'll give it to you right away."

He looked at me, his expression somber and resolute, got up from the table, and held four fingers in front of my face. "I need this much. If you can get it to me, I'll let you ride me like a donkey."

"Four hundred grand?" I asked. I was relieved—nowadays, four hundred thousand wasn't really that large a sum. "No problem. I'll get it right away. I've got it at home."

But he shook his head. "Add a zero!"

"Four million?" I tried not to gape at him. "Shit, you really impress the hell out of me. Did you turn into Bill Gates in prison? Why do you need so much for this expedition?"

"Stop asking so many questions. Just understand that I need this much money. Do you have it or not?"

From the expression on my face, Lao Yang knew I was shocked. He refilled my wine glass once more and said, "I knew you didn't have it, right? If it were only four hundred thousand, I wouldn't have had to come to you, brother!"

"Don't draw conclusions so fast. I can go and see if I can raise it. But first you have to tell me why you need that much."

"Raise it how? Who are you going to borrow it from? I know all of your friends and none of them has that kind of money. As for why I need it, I can't tell you that yet—only that once it's in my hands, I'll be able to resolve a matter of life and death."

Lao Yang was absolutely dead-on correct. Few of my friends would be able to lend me any money at all, let alone a small fortune, and if I asked my old man, that skinflint just might kill me. It wasn't going to be easy, coming up with four million.

Lao Yang patted me on the back and said in the most patronizing tones I had ever heard from anyone in my entire life, "Come now, let's not talk about money anymore. The best I can hope for is to persuade you to come with me on this adventure. After all, it won't be your first time as a grave robber—it's not that big a deal. As a matter of fact, this shouldn't even be thought of as grave robbing. We'll go to that pit where the sacrificial victims were buried. You'll help me choose the things that are worth something and bypass the ones without value. There's nothing illegal about picking up what you accidentally find through good fortune. We'll pretend we're tourists, there to admire the beautiful mountains and rivers—and the luscious figures of those mountain girls. Come on—you don't have a girlfriend—maybe you'll find yourself a wife to keep you warm in your old age."

I didn't have the patience to listen to his bullshit and shook my head. "You really make it sound easy. Are there truly things worth four million in that place you've babbled about? If you want to recoup that sum and make a profit besides, you'd have to find a tomb from the Han dynasty, and they've already been picked clean. You're wasting your time and you think you can trick me into wasting mine—and my money too."

"Damn it, do you think I'm so stupid I didn't think about that? I'll tell you what: I won't be rushing down to that same old burial pit when I return. My cousin told me that near the place where we went last time, close to the burial pit, there's a gigantic royal tomb. That's my goal this time. Let's go and have a look. With your grave-robbing experience, I think we're certain to find this tomb and a fortune for each of us too."

"Go look for someone else. If you're headed for an ancient tomb, I definitely don't want to go."

"Don't wimp out on me—are we brothers or not? Just think about this: you can help me and you can continue to investigate your Uncle Three's disappearance. Believe it or not, my venture here is connected to your uncle; even if you don't give a damn about helping me, think of your uncle. You really owe it to him to come with me."

With the mention of my uncle, my heart plunged. I thought of the strange relationship between the earring Lao Yang had found and the bells in the cavern of the blood zombies and in the undersea tomb where my uncle had gone missing. Lao Yang was right. The clues about Uncle Three's fate were heartbreakingly scarce. The hexagonal bells were one of the very few leads I might ever have. If I didn't grab this opportunity, who knows if I would ever find my uncle?

But when I thought about my past two grave-robbing adventures, my feet began to ache. I was scared and I really didn't want the toil and pain of climbing mountains. I had come home to rest and relax and resume the life of an indolent and honest man.

I hesitated and then made a snap decision. If I were going to live with myself in the future, I had to go on this adventure with Lao Yang, for the sake of our friendship as well as for Uncle Three. I could go, assess the situation, and refuse to take part in it if it seemed unsound and life-threatening.

And to be honest, I was curious about this proposal. The minute I decided to embark upon it, I felt sure I had made the right choice.

"Okay. Since you put it that way, I'll go with you, Lao Yang. But first you have to give me your earring. I'll go and find out what dynasty it's from and whether it's worth anything. If it's not, that will prove that this place isn't worth investigating and you'll have to make other plans."

Once he knew I was going to help, Lao Yang was willing to do whatever I wanted. "Okay. Take it—if you really want it, it's yours forever."

"But let me warn you," I said, glaring at his grinning face, "you have to listen to everything I say after we get to this place. Even if you need to fart, you'll have to get my okay before you stink up the air, got it?"

Lao Yang was gone; his heart had already flown to the Qinling Mountains and he was ready to say anything to keep me there with him. "Of course, of course. As long as we take four million yuan with us, you can be my mother and father come back to life and rolled into one. As far as farting goes, come with me and you can fart in my face whenever you want to."

With that he fell flat on the tabletop, drunk and snoring. I stood up to help him to his feet, lost my balance, and woke up the next morning under the restaurant's table.

We were busy men that month. Since I had been ready to give up grave robbing, I'd sold all of my equipment, so I made a list and sent Lao Yang to purchase what we needed. Then I flew back to Jinan with Fats's fish- eye stone to visit Lao Hai, the old man in the antique market who had given me such a good price for Uncle Three's jade burial shroud.

After Lao Hai peered at the fish-eye gem, he looked a bit worried. "Oh, master, I sell antiques," he said. "You should take this to a jeweler and let him give you a price for it."

"This rock is an antique. It's at least four to five hundred years old."

Still smiling, he said, "I know that, but what you bring me has to be recognizably ancient. If this stone were set into a hairpin or a brooch, it would be a treasure. But how am I supposed to sell it in its raw state? Even if you said it was an antique, no one would believe you. How about this—I'll find a jade hairpin for you. We'll fit this orb on it and see if it'll sell. I'll give you a deposit and you leave it here with me. Those who can tell the good from the bad will offer a good price."

He was sincere, and I didn't have time to haggle. I accepted his deposit of a quarter million yuan and returned to Hangzhou feeling a bit depressed. Then I took the earring Lao Yang gave me and visited a friend of my grandfather's, the only man who might know about the origin of this bell and whether it was worth anything.

Mr. Qi was the first antique dealer to set up shop in Hangzhou. Now he was recognized widely as an authority on Chinese history and served as a guest professor at several universities. His expertise and knowledge were augmented by his research, especially about the minority populations in China. When I handed the bell to him, I could see his eyes narrow and his hands begin to tremble.

蛇神

CHAPTER THREE

THE LOST KINGDOM

Mr. Qi examined the bell for at least three hours and flipped through six or seven books that were as thick as bricks before he lifted his head and looked at me. He sighed. "I'm embarrassed. I've never seen anything like this before, even though I've been studying minority cultures for years. Where did you find this?"

I had to answer but it was impossible to tell him the truth. I made up a story from some of the main points I had heard from Lao Yang, and Mr. Qi's eyes gleamed as I spoke.

"Do you think it's valuable?" I asked, and he sighed.

"This bell could have been made as long ago as the Western Zhou dynasty. The pattern on it is called the double-bodied serpent with a human face. It probably came from an ancient country called the She Kingdom, which suddenly disappeared two thousand years ago. It was at its peak during the early Western Zhou dynasty. Then in a matter of ten to twenty years, its entire civilization vanished into the jungle."

"It is spoken of in many myths and legends as the Serpent Kingdom," he continued. "The word She sounded the same as the word serpent and the people of She treated the double-bodied serpent with a human face as a divinity, so this design was often found on many of their adornments. Because information about it comes from ancient texts, not everyone is aware that the She Kingdom ever existed. In the world of antique dealers, this bell would be inconsequential, but for those who know about the kingdom, it would be priceless."

I felt a little sick when I heard this. Even if we could bring out treasures from the tombs Lao Yang was sure were waiting for us, they would be almost impossible to sell. It looked as though this trip would be a waste of time.

Mr. Qi saw my disappointment. "Is there a problem?" he asked. Since I knew he was a merchant as well as a scholar, I told him that I needed to sell the earring to raise four million yuan fast.

He thought for a minute in silence and then patted my shoulder. "If you want to sell this earring, I can help you find a good buyer. Four million is absolutely not a problem. But you can't tell anyone about this."

I understood. This revered old man was actually a member of the underworld, working on the kind of business deals that had flourished pre-liberation. But it was no skin off my ass so long as he was going to make the contacts and handle the sale. I smiled, nodded, and thanked him in tones of formal politeness, which was more than the old reprobate deserved.

Before I left him, Mr. Qi gave me several books about the She Kingdom. I flipped through them and saw pictures of murals that showed a large group of people praying in front of a tree that was covered with corpses dangling from its branches. Captions below explained that the most important festival in the She Kingdom was the worship of the "Serpent God Tree." According to legends, if men sacrificed fresh blood to it, any wish they made would come true. The tree's shape looked a lot like the drawing that Lao Yang had made; could the bronze tree that he dug up be some sort of replica of the Serpent God Tree?

There was a pattern of the human-faced serpent in many of the murals, and also the same sort of bells that we had found in both the cavern of the blood zombies as well as at the undersea tomb. I couldn't remember whether they were embellished with the double-bodied serpent with a human face, but judging by their shapes, the bells in these three places must have come from the same place. This mysterious She Kingdom might be the key to unlocking my puzzle, I thought.

Two days later, I was lying on a bed of a long-distance sleeper bus to Xian, next to the one where Lao Yang rested. As we chatted, Lao Yang asked, "Do you want to go to other places, not just the pit I found three years ago? After all, it's not easy to go into the mountains and we shouldn't waste this chance. Wouldn't it be great if we could find other tombs nearby?

I'd already planned on doing this. This area could be within the range of the ancient serpent kingdom. Anything we found there might be enormously helpful in discovering the link between the other places I'd been and this spot. But I didn't want to talk it over with Lao Yang—at least not yet. "Don't be greedy," I laughed. "You might not remember your way back to where you were. What will you do if you can't even take me to that famous pit of yours?"

"Oh, but I left my mark there," Lao Yang boasted, and I laughed even harder.

"It's been three years. What kind of mark will stay in place after three years of mountain weather?"

"Just wait and see. Forget three years, you'll be able to see my mark in another thirty years."

I was too drowsy to pay any attention to his bragging. The motion of the bus began to feel like the rocking of a hammock and I fell fast asleep.

It was dark when we got to Xian. We had dinner, wandered through the night market, and then settled down for a beer. Sure that our southern dialect would be incomprehensible to the people around us, we talked openly about our journey until we were interrupted by an old man sitting beside us. He grinned as he asked, "Gentlemen, are you here to do some business in local products?"

CHAPTER FOUR

ON THE TRACK

At first we had trouble understanding his heavy accent when he spoke our dialect, but Lao Yang deciphered his words and asked, "What do you mean?"

The old man switched to Mandarin and asked, "I mean are you guys going to do business? Are you coming to dig up some local products?"

"We—we're just traveling here," Lao Yang answered. "Why do you ask, old man, do you want to sell us local specialties of some kind?"

The old man laughed, waved his hand, and walked away, leaving the two of us puzzled. We heard him say to the people he was sitting with, "It's all right, don't worry. Just two innocent virgins who aren't going up into the hills. They don't know anything. No need to fuss over them."

Lao Yang's face began to twitch a little and he said quietly, "Let's get out of here now." Confused by his change of mood, I put ten yuan on the table and we walked away. Once we reached the corner of the road, I asked, "Why did we have to leave? We only drank half of our beer."

Lao Yang glanced back to the stall rather furtively and said, "That—that old man. Just now he said to the people at the same table that we were two virgins. I heard this sort of jargon before when I was in prison. Going up into the hills is the slang used by grave robbers here when they talk about their trade. Virgins mean that we're not people in the business. That group seems fishy to me; I'm sure they came to Xian for the same reason we did. They heard us talking about grave robbing and came over to listen in."

"We didn't have to leave, did we? Seems a bit extreme to me—after all, what could they do to us in a beer stall?"

Lao Yang patted my back and said, "You can't understand unless you've been in prison. It's hard to explain the underworld unless you've been around people who work in it. I'm sure that those guys eavesdropped on every word we said, although it sounds as though they didn't understand much of it. If they know about the tomb we're looking for, we could be in real trouble here."

Heaven only knows what kind of exaggerated bullshit Lao Yang had been told by other prisoners. I thought it was better not to argue with him so we went back to our hotel room and rested for our journey the next day.

We were up well before daybreak, with thirty pounds of equipment and supplies on each of our backs. It was quite early when we began our journey on a small bus toward China's largest mountain range.

We traveled along a highway for three hours, finally reaching Mount Changyang, where we turned toward the source of the Jialing River.

I was accustomed to driving on straight roads. But there was one small turn every five seconds and a big one every ten seconds on the mountain roads here. I rested my head on the seat before me and felt like all of my guts were turning upside down.

Lao Yang was in even worse shape. He hadn't been in a vehicle for three years, except for the large, comfortable bus that had brought us to Xian, and even that had made him queasy. For him, this ride was sheer hell. Struggling to keep from vomiting, he said, "I'm old, I'm real old. Old people are useless. Three years ago I could just manage to make this journey and this time I can't even keep my eyelids open."

"Shut up, damn it, this route was your idea. You didn't want to take the highway. You had to go out of the way to take these windy roads next to the hills. It's no use whining about it now."

He waved my words aside and muttered, "If you talk to me again, I know I'm going to puke. Just leave me to my misery, will you?"

Before he could close his mouth there was a huge explosive crash that rattled the windows of our little bus. I peered out and saw a gigantic cloud of dust blotting out the sky.

"What—what's that?" Lao Yang stuttered. "Earthquake?"

A middle-aged man sitting in front of us turned around and smiled. "The two of you aren't from around here, are you? That's someone bombing a tomb. There are always two or three of these bombs going off every day at this time of year."

Confused, I asked, "Who would dare to rob a grave in broad daylight?"

He grinned, exposing a mouthful of yellow teeth. "The mountain on the opposite side of the river is different from the one over here. We have these windy roads along the hills here, but on that side there's no road at all. Even if you called the police now, it would take them at least one day and one night to get to the site of the explosion. Unless you grew wings and flew over there, you can only hear the destruction, unable to stop it."

I nodded, still confused. "These things go on without interference?"

The man laughed. "This could be considered a special feature of our area, especially during this season. A group of robbers was caught a couple days ago. But there are fewer and fewer ancient tombs now. It's just not worth it to go to all this trouble anymore the way it was a few years ago. There may be more tombs in the remote mountains, but it's too difficult to get to them. Even the government has to turn a blind eye to whatever goes on in the boondocks over there."

I muttered "I see" and turned to look out the window. All I could see was a luxuriant and boundless forest. It was impossible to get a glimpse of what lay under its dense, green canopy.

I had done some research before we started our journey. The Qinling Mountain range within Shanxi province was spread in a wasp shape. The wings of the east and west mountains were separated by many smaller ranges. The mountains and valleys were arranged one after the other with many deep rivers flowing through. The eight-hundred-mile Qin River was a famous landmark containing many cultural ruins from ancient times, especially on its northern slopes where lay countless imperial tombs and gigantic burial sites of officials and wealthy men.

Naturally this was a place that had always attracted hordes of grave robbers. I simply didn't expect that those robbers would brazenly bomb grave sites without going into the deepest parts of the Qinling Mountains. Evidently, it wouldn't be easy to find one or two tombs close at hand that would be worth robbing at all.

My informant was quite enthusiastic; once the topic was disclosed, he didn't want to stop discussing it. He handed me a cigarette and asked, "Did you guys come to sightsee? Where do you want to go?"

"We want to go and take a look at Mount Taibai," I replied, and he nodded. "You can't go far if you don't hire a tour guide. There are so many twists and bends in the trails that it's easy to lose your way. Do you want me to go with you? I live in the village on the edge of the protected area. You'll get there after we pass two more mountains. You'll see, you'll need a tour guide when you come out here to hike around."

I had a feeling that this guy might be dangerous; mountainfolk are known for being bandits. He could take us out to the ravines and then stab us to death. I hastily shook my head. "No need, there's no need. We've made our own arrangements."

"Don't shake your head so soon," the man said. "This place is unlike any other. The mountain forests are as thick as jungles and if you two go in alone, you could be in a lot of danger. Think it over. I'm quite well known as a guide and I know what I'm talking about. I'm not trying to scare you just so I can make a few yuan."

He sounded sincere and I felt embarrassed at my city suspicions. "We've come here to spend time with the ethnic minorities in the villages around here," I lied. "First we'll stay in the foothills for a few days, so we're in no rush to hire a guide. When we're ready to set off into the mountains, we'll come looking for you."

"I'm afraid you'll still need a guide, even to study the minorities. To get to the nearest Yao village, you have to cross this mountain." He pointed to the mountain range in a distance. "This is called Mount Serpent Head and its peak is more than three thousand feet above sea level. Look, you can see the whole mountain looks like the head of a serpent, so that's what we call it. Many people have died on this mountain. Some students from the arts college went in by themselves to sketch nature's wonders last year, and they still haven't come out. Believe me, you need a guide."

I could see Mount Serpent Head stretching across the horizon, richly green with cloud-capped peaks. The rest of the mountain range was so mist-shrouded I could only see cliffs, so steep that not even a monkey could scale them. As I stared, I wondered if I could survive an attempt to climb this range.

After another hour, finally we reached the foot of Mount Taibai. Lao Yang and I staggered off the bus and my new friend the tour guide insisted upon recommending a hotel for us. I thought now that we were on his turf, we should listen to his advice, so we followed along. He checked us into a small hotel that looked clean and had low prices; this guy is genuinely warm-hearted, I decided, and all of my misgivings about him vanished.

After he saw that we were settled in, he cupped his hand in front of his chest to say goodbye. He gave us his phone number before he left, telling us to be sure to give him a call when we were ready to go into the mountains and he would take us there safely.

The owner of the hotel was a hospitable and talkative lady who insisted that she would make dinner for us. We were too embarrassed to eat with her in her private living quarters so Lao Yang and I went back to our room, leaned against the windowsill, and studied a map of the area as we ate some of our own provisions.

The guide had told me the truth. From here, we would need to climb a three-thousand-foot mountain to get to the heart of the Qinling Mountain forest. With our lack of experience, it would be suicide for us to go into the mountains alone, but if we asked that guide to take us in, he would want to take us out as well. It would be okay for him to wait for us for a couple of days but it might take us over a week to poke around in there, and he was sure to become suspicious.

The last time that Lao Yang was here, his cousin found a retired grave robber to guide them. Now that his cousin wasn't around, it would probably be impossible to find this guide again.

Lao Yang had never thought he would return when he first made the trip, so he had practically no memory of the roads. We asked the owner if there was a route other than going over the mountain, but she said there was no alternative. Usually the locals came to her village to go to the market, and they always climbed over the mountain to get here. She had never heard of any kind of shortcut, she told us, looking puzzled that we would ask.

As I sat wondering what we should do, Lao Yang tapped me on the shoulder and murmured, "Quick—come and look. Who do you see down there?"

I peeked out the window and saw that five people had entered the hotel courtyard. One of the five was the old man who had questioned us at the beer stall in Xian.

Why were these people here? Had Lao Yang been right? Were they on the same quest that we were? My mind whirred with unanswered questions.

Lao Yang closed the curtain, leaving only a small peephole. He whispered, "These guys are carrying bags of equipment, just like us. Could they have followed us from Xian to get to the ancient tomb before we do?"

I shook my head as I saw the owner of the hotel go out to welcome them, smiling as she approached. "No, it doesn't look like that. You see how the hotel owner is greeting them? I think these people probably are regular customers. There aren't too many places to stay around here. It's probably just a coincidence that we ended up at the same hotel."

Lao Yang frowned. "I don't think you're right. They heard us talking in Xian. If they see us here, there's no guarantee they won't want to get a jump on us by leaving tonight."

I shook my head and said, "No. Actually we can use them to our advantage, no matter what their business might be. You and I have no experience in this part of the world—we might as well follow them rather than charge over that mountain on our own. For one thing, we can see if they're searching for treasures and for another, we can follow them over the mountain in safety."

"I'm sure these guys are outlaws," Lao Yang argued. "Killing us would be no big deal for them. If they find out that we're following them, we'll be dead men. Your plan is too risky."

"When did you become such a fussy old lady? We're not fools. We can run if we think they have a clue that we're stalking them. If you're really worried, we can follow them for a short distance and see how alert they are. If they seem suspicious, we'll come back here. There's nothing to lose, right?"

Lao Yang nodded with no more argument; we packed in preparation for an early departure in the morning and went to bed.

We overslept. I leaped to my feet when I saw the sun high in the sky at noon and ran downstairs to ask about the five guys we planned to follow. "Oh they're already on their way, bound for Mount Serpent Head," the owner told me, "but they didn't leave too long before you got up."

Lao Yang and I rushed off to catch up with them; racing fast for half an hour, we finally caught sight of them at the foot of Mount Serpent Head.

CHAPTER FIVE

ON THE TRAIL

At the bottom of Mount Serpent Head were paved roads leading to sightseeing spots, so in the beginning climbing wasn't a strain. The roads meandered past mountain streams, cliff carvings, and statues of famous people; the scenery was spectacular. But the group we were tailing moved rapidly and paid no attention to the beauty that they walked through.

The mountain became increasingly quiet as we walked along. We were silent as well, not daring to talk in case we drew the attention of the men that we followed. Darkness fell but our group didn't stop for the night until the moon reached the middle of the sky.

We squatted down in the bushes and watched them from our hiding place. Lao Yang tugged on my sleeve and when I turned I saw his face was pale and sweaty. He was in poor physical condition after his stint in prison and I was sure he was dehydrated as well as exhausted. This is going to be fun, mountain climbing with a guy who has no stamina, I thought, but smiled as patiently as I could and handed him an emergency canteen of water.

As he gasped for breath, Lao Yang whispered, "I think we should forget—forget about following these guys. Let them carry off what they find and we'll look for our own treasure. I'll die if we keep following them at this pace."

I knew he was right but hearing him voice my thoughts pissed me off. "How the hell did you get to be such a useless piece of shit after three years in prison? If we stop following them now, then all the exertion we just went through would be wasted effort. Shut up, grit your teeth, and hang in there."

"How long do you think they're going to keep going?" Lao Yang asked. "Do you think they've stopped because they've reached their destination?"

I glanced at the group and said, "No. This place isn't deep enough into the mountain. You see, they've started a fire; they're going to spend the night here, so let's fill our bellies and get some sleep."

We made a makeshift campsite in the bushes; a campfire would give us away so we ate our food cold and shivered in our sweat-dampened clothes.

"Damn, what a lousy way to spend the night," Lao Yang complained and I muttered, "Right, prison must have been so much better, hmm? If you can't rough it, then let's go back and forget the whole thing. Better to turn back now before we waste any more time."

"Fuck you," he mumbled. "We don't even know if these guys plan to climb the mountain. What are we going to do if they just roam around in the forest?"

He was right. Just because they were headed in the direction we wanted to go didn't mean they were going to lead us to the area where we wanted to end up. And we could hardly go over and ask them where they were going. Not only did I have no reply, I had no big ideas of what to do either.

"You see, you're the one who's useless. I'm the one to rely on. I'm going to sneak over and listen in on what they're saying. They have to be discussing their plans for tomorrow—it's only logical."

"Terrific, you're the mastermind, jailbird. But I'm not going to let you go over there alone." And together we began to crawl through the darkness toward the light of the blazing campfire.

We hadn't gone far before we could hear voices, and Lao Yang beckoned to me that we should stop. We hugged the ground and held our breath as we heard a voice whine, "Uncle Tai. Can you give us an idea of how long it's going to take to get to our destination. My legs are almost dead from today's walk."

A hoarse voice replied, "I told you to exercise a bit more before we started this trek but all you ever did was eat, drink, whore around, and gamble. The only workout you ever got was on some girl's mattress—serves you right if your muscles ache now. We have at least two more days on this road before we climb Mount Serpent Head. But I don't know how long it will take us after we reach the spot where the road ends. If you can't take it, go back now. I don't want anyone coming along who can't keep up with me."

"Hey, I didn't mean to say I don't want to keep going. Don't worry, Uncle. If we make a good haul on this trip, then this is our last time, right? We can go to Hong Kong with Boss Wang and Boss Lee with money to burn and we'll live like rich men, isn't that the truth?"

A voice with a Cantonese accent said, "Yes, yes. We've already discussed this; as long as you guys take care of business, we'll give you cash for everything you can find. This is going to be the sale of a lifetime. If we all do a good job, then every one of us can retire in Hong Kong where there are a thousand places for you to spend your money. You'll know this little bit of hardship was all worthwhile once you're living a fat life in the city."

"We're not the only ones responsible for the success of this expedition, Boss Lee," the man called Uncle Tai grumbled. "Whether this grave is in the place where we're headed depends on what you've told us. If your information is false, none of us will get what we want."

"Shit, Old Tai, you're such a skeptic. We've worked together for a long time—when did I ever steer you wrong? To be honest, once we get to this place, you guys won't want to leave it even if I promised to show you where you could dig up the First Emperor's grave."

"I don't believe your bullshit," Uncle Tai sneered. "Don't promise anything that you don't know is a sure thing. Yes, we've been working together for a long time but I still don't know where you got your current information. Let us know what's going on here."

"Yeah, give us some background," yelled the man who had just complained of weariness.

Mr. Lee laughed. "You two really amuse me. If you want to know, I can tell you but I don't think you'll believe what I have to say."

CHAPTER SIX

EAVESDROPPING

For a few minutes we heard nothing until Mr. Lee said, "Well, I didn't plan to tell anyone this, but we've all worked together for so long that I think of you as family. Since you want to know all about what we're headed into, I'll give you a quick rundown."

Uncle Tai's nephew broke in. "Great. Tell me, do you have a special way to find exactly where a tomb is located on the first try?"

"There's nothing special about my methods nor are they a secret. They've been passed down my family tree for generations. Let me tell you. During the time of turmoil and chaos in the Northern Wei dynasty, countless battles were fought every day and many men died fighting. My great-great-grandfather was only six years old, but he had to tend a herd of cattle in order to feed his family.

"Riots broke out near his village that year. The troops came to suppress the unrest, and the people in the village fled. My family ran out of time and couldn't escape before the troops came, so they were trapped inside their house. Outside the killings went on and the skies were shrouded with gloom. The bloodshed continued for three days straight before things quieted down again.

"With fear and trepidation, my great-great-grandfather sneaked outside and found the streets covered with bodies, many near death but still breathing. He was only six, remember, so he was terrified by what he saw. He ran to look for his cattle, but when he got to the pen where they were kept, all of his cows were gone. Lying in the straw and mud was a wounded soldier.

"The soldier was a deaf-mute who was nearly dead. My great-great-grandfather felt sorry for the man, brought him water, and wiped the blood from his wounds with his own shirt. But it was no use; the soldier died within minutes of being found.

"Before he stopped breathing, he reached inside his shirt, took out a roll of linen that was covered with words, gave it to the boy who had helped him, and gestured that he should take good care of it.

"Unfortunately, everyone in my family was illiterate in those days and had no way of knowing what was written on the linen. That winter was horribly cold, and many people froze to death. My great-great-grandfather's mother saved her family by using the piece of linen and some bits of old cotton to make quilted undershirts that helped fend off the bitter weather.

"The boy grew up, joined the army, and was brave enough to be promoted eventually to a military commander. But it was a volatile period in history, and dynasties rose and fell quickly. By the time he was old, my great-great-grandfather no longer had power or influence, and when he died, he was buried with nothing more valuable than that old piece of quilted linen that he had been given so long ago.

"Long afterward, our family relocated to another part of

the country and when they moved the ancestral graves to their new home, servants were careless with my great-great-grandfather's coffin, spilling his bones onto the ground. After picking up the skeleton, my grandfather found that everything inside had decomposed except for a piece of linen which was still extremely well preserved.

"Curious about the cloth, my grandfather showed it to someone in the family who had an antique business. At one glance, the relative knew that the linen was special, inscribed with words that were called the Language of the Mutes. According to folklore, this was a written language that could only be read by deaf-mutes."

Mr. Lee stopped here and asked, "Does anyone know what this language was?"

Again there was silence and then a voice that had not yet spoken said, "I was told about this by my uncle. There was an army of deaf-mutes at the time of the Northern Wei dynasty and they used linen like this to pass on secret information that was written in this language. Few other people could understand it."

Mr. Lee nodded and said, "Liang is masterful indeed. Do you know what this army did?"

Liang laughed. "I'm not quite sure. But I heard that although people were told they were the emperor's guards, secretly they were an army of grave robbers. Because they were deaf-mutes and used the Language of the Mutes that only they could understand, nobody but the emperor and they themselves knew the locations of the tombs that they looted. Their lives and discoveries have always been steeped in mystery."

He paused here and asked, "Mr. Lee, did the piece of linen

you're talking about hold the secret locations of the tombs?"

Mr. Lee laughed. "You're right."

"Your family could have made a fortune with that."

"What are you talking about? I don't understand," Tai's nephew complained.

"According to legend," Liang began, "after the army of deaf-mutes found a tomb, first they recorded the location before excavation. They rode horseback over the spot to flatten the surface and then poured molten lead on the level ground. When they were ready to begin digging, their written record led them back to the tomb, and that record was written on the Lee family's piece of linen."

"That's true," Mr. Lee said. "The cloth in my great-great-grandfather's coffin documents the locations of twenty-four ancient tombs. We've been to all but the one we're heading to now and this last one should be the best of all."

"Does the cloth tell what's inside the tomb?"

"No, the records aren't that detailed. But it mentions one of the treasures in this grave, which is three times more amazing than the mausoleum of the First Emperor. Believe me, this tomb is going to make us all fabulously rich."

So Lao Yang and I were right—this group was in the same business we were—but they had an historical relic on their side.

"Do you think that what Lee said was—was real? There is really a grave in this world that's better than the First Emperor, Qin Shi Huang's mausoleum?" Lao Yang was so excited that his stammer was worse than ever.

"That guy is dead serious—I'm sure it's at least partially true. What I'm certain of is they're going to climb the mountain tomorrow and we're going to tag along behind."

"Then we—we might as well follow them to the end. Let's not go to my sacrificial pit—we'll just go after them instead, okay?"

His stutter and his excitement made him forget to lower his voice and I quickly covered his mouth to shut him up. But it was already too late. The group had stopped talking and I was sure they had heard Lao Yang.

We held our breaths, trying not to make a sound, but our hearts were pounding so loud I was sure that would give us away. The group was dead silent until Uncle Tai whispered, "Pockmark, that was a weird noise—go check it out."

I could hear the sounds of a pistol being loaded. Just our luck to follow a band of killers, I thought, and just my luck to travel with this idiot, Lao Yang. I turned to see what our escape options were—it looked as though we might have an eighty percent chance of getting away in one piece if we took off. We'd be in trouble if they decided to track us down but if we didn't run now, we were sure to die.

As we hesitated, a burst of noise came from the distance and I could see four or five flashlights coming closer.

"Mountain security patrol," Lao Yang whispered just as Uncle Tai murmured, "Damn, let's go." The five of them quickly stamped out their fire, grabbed their bags, and ran off into the forest.

"What—what should we do? Should we chase—chase after them or not?" Lao Yang quavered.

I cautiously peeked out from our hiding place and saw only darkness; none of the fleeing five had turned on their flashlights. The forest had swallowed up even their shadows.

"That's not possible," I explained. "You see how dark it is? If we chase after them, we might end up getting ahead of them. Let's just take a break and track them down in the morning. They won't have gotten very far; they need to rest as much as we do."

Lao Yang realized we had no other choice but to wait; the patrol was close by and we had to move to another spot. "Shut up and follow me," I hissed at Lao Yang and led the way into the forest. We found a thicket of bushes and crouched down as we watched the flashlights of the patrol team fade from sight.

I thought for a little while and said, "The locals have said that now is the high season for grave robbing. I'm afraid there will be patrols out all night long and we're not going to sleep too soundly. Let's find a place to rest for one night and then hit the trail full speed tomorrow. If we get caught tonight how are we going to explain why we're here to a patrol?"

Lao Yang kept nodding but when I looked closely at him, I realized it wasn't because he agreed with me but because he was dozing off. I sighed and pulled my shirt close to my shivering body. It looked like I was the one who would have the first watch on guard duty. But when I leaned against a tree, I began to feel drowsy, and fell asleep.

We woke up early the next day. Because we were sleeping under the trees, our heads were covered with bird shit and the stink of it almost made me puke. Lao Yang was unconcerned and just brushed the shit from his hair with his hand, which made me even more nauseated. There was no way I was going to run around with my head in this condition so I washed my hair with a bottle of water.

I followed Lao Yang as we rushed back to the place where we had been the night before, and I prayed there might be some clues left behind that would help us know more about our quarry. But after walking around in circles, we couldn't even find the ashes from their bonfire. Lao Yang kept nagging, "That's why I said we should follow—follow them last night. Isn't this great? Even the cooked duck has flown away."

I'd had enough. "God damn it. Stop your bitching. There's only one road here. Where could they have gone? Just keep moving and we'll find them."

We raced to catch up with the group but after walking all morning, we came to the road's end without finding any trace of the five men. If we kept going, we would soon enter a forest where the trees were as tall as the sky and thick bushes obscured the ground.

There was no trace of other people and I began to feel worried and a bit scared. The absence of signs meant we were beyond the realm of the safety patrol, and that was a mixed blessing. Nobody to catch us meant nobody to rescue us. Now we were on the edge of true wilderness and I tried not to think of how many cliffs lay ahead that we would have to climb.

We still had found no evidence of a recent campfire, which meant the group hadn't taken time to rest after they fled the patrol but had traveled all night. This meant we didn't have a hope in hell of catching them.

I hesitated at the end of the road and then plunged toward a decision. There were limits to any human's energy. If these people had spent the whole night running, they would have to rest today. And in the darkness they would have traveled much more slowly than they had during the day. They couldn't be too far ahead of us and I was sure we could still catch up with them. Our only worry was to be stealthy and silent so they didn't get a hint of our presence as we drew near.

I took a hunting knife from my backpack and hung it on my belt. Each of us snapped a large branch from a tree to use as a walking stick. We knew there were wild beasts in these mountain forests, tigers, bears, wolves, and wild boars. If we blundered into any of them, Lao Yang and I would be enough food to last them for a couple of days.

"What are we going to do if we don't catch up with Mr. Lee and his gang by tonight?" Lao Yang asked.

"According to what I read before we set off on this little jaunt of ours, people who come here to hunt for herbs build little huts and stock them with firewood and dried food for emergencies. If we can find one of those, then we'll have a real rest this evening and we can make plans after that."

"Maybe we should turn back. Look at what we're about to enter. There's nothing here, not even a ghost's shadow. We'll die if we get lost in this forest—hundreds of people already have. You remember what the poet Li Bai said, "The roads of Shu are difficult to travel."

"Listen to you," I scoffed. "Where's the tough jailbird who first came up with this scheme? I think you're only tough when you're looking at the bottom of a bottle. Before we even get into the mountains, you're giving me the whole roads-of-Shu-are-difficult-to-take bullshit. If you insist, we'll turn back, but don't ever mention the words 'grave robbing' to me again."

Lao Yang smiled and said, "I'm only testing you by talking this way. It looks as though you've really gone from being a bookworm to joining the hoodlums and scoundrels of the world. As one of them, let me welcome you to our midst—and don't worry. The last thing I'll ever do is turn back from this adventure. We're going together and we'll come back rich."

The forest could only be entered by hacking a trail through the bushes, and it was hard to find our footing. The ground was covered with tussocks of tall grass and the treetops made a sky of dark green above us, blocking out the sun. The lack of light gave a confusing tinge to everything we passed through.

Just as I was certain that we had been walking through the same area over and over, going in circles, our steps began to go up a steep incline and we saw a cliff in front of us. A narrow pathway made from a single plank was the only way up, looking none too stable. It was wrapped in periwinkle vines and covered with green slime that made me wonder if it had rotted away. I didn't want to think of how long it had been in place or when was the last time anyone had set foot on it.

"Hey there! What are you guys doing anyway?" Approaching us through the forest was a group of men and women, one of whom called out to greet us. "Wait! We're headed this way too, going to the village on the other side of this mountain."

Lao Yang and I quickly tucked our knives out of sight and went to meet our fellow travelers. "Brothers and sisters, we're tourists from another part of the country, heading for the same village. How long will that take, could you please tell us?"

A woman in a long red gown looked at us sternly and asked. "Our village? Why would you want to come to our tumbledown community anyway?"

She looked sharp-witted so I put on a meek and shy expression. "I've come to visit an old man I met there two years ago. He was kind to me and let me stay in his home so I wanted to come back and thank him. But two years is a long time and now I don't remember how to get to his village."

"Nonsense," the woman scolded me. "You're a thief if I ever saw one. The look on your face would let a half-wit know what you have in mind—if you're not a grave robber, you're a poacher of wild game. Think you can fool me? You're not that clever, my lad."

I stared at her, shocked and speechless, but Lao Yang pushed his way past me and put one hundred yuan in the woman's hand. "Here, quit—quit your babble. Which one of your eyes saw us robbing a grave? Please answer me politely, if you can. This hundred yuan is yours if you shut your mouth. Otherwise, keep yapping away and you'll feel my hand slapping your face."

There were several brawny men in this group and once I heard what Lao Yang said, I thought we were doomed. Mountain people are ferocious and proud and they don't put up with outsiders telling them what to do. I took a step backward and got ready to run. But a man standing behind the suspicious old harpy plucked the money from Lao Yang's hand and smiled.

"Don't be angry, my wife was just joking. You have to go to the left if you want to go to our village. Walk around the mountain until you come to a waterfall. Continue walking straight ahead along the stream. That's the fastest shortcut. As long as you follow the stream, you'll definitely get to our village."

Lao Yang grinned and said, "You're lying. Isn't it faster if we walk up this plank pathway?"

"We don't know when this path was built. It's never been repaired and none of us dare to walk on it now," the man told us. He glanced up at the sky.

"Ah. I think you guys won't be able to get there by this evening. You'll have to spend the night in the mountains. There are a few streams shooting off from the main river and if you're not familiar with the place, you could easily follow the wrong fork. Why don't we do this—we came to gather some pigweed over here. You guys wait for us. Tomorrow we'll return to the village, and you can come too. That way you'll be okay." Then he came over to help me carry my gear.

He seemed friendly enough and I made some quick mental calculations. The place we were heading for was in the valley on the opposite side of Mount Serpent Head. It had already taken us almost three days to get to this point. It had been impossible for us to carry more than a week's worth of food and we'd certainly need to stop at the next village to buy more supplies. The five people in front of us were long gone, and humans were scarce in this corner of the earth. With the help of these villagers, we no longer faced the risk of getting lost in the mountains.

Lao Yang and I looked at each other and then nodded. "In that case, big brother, thank you. Here, please take these," I said as I took out some cigarettes.

That gabby old woman opened her mouth to start in on us again, but after one look from her husband, she scowled at us in silence.

Among the mountain people, men were generally the

heads of the households while the women kept quiet, so as long as we were on good terms with her husband, this old biddy had no choice but to put up with us. Every time I caught sight of her unhappy face, I had to struggle to keep from snickering.

We walked for an hour or so until we reached a meadow, and the villagers all began to gather plants as we tried to assess the terrain that we would soon pass through. The mountains that we could see were like foothills, green and plush and round as pillows. I wondered where Lao Yang's burial pit was and how long it would be before we found it.

It was evening before the villagers stopped work, and Lao Yang and I each picked up a bag of pigweed that was almost as big as we were, but luckily much lighter. We trudged along with the setting sun behind us; as the sky turned to a faded deep blue, Lao Yang became more and more alert.

"What's on your mind?" I asked and he replied, "I've been here before. We're coming to a rest stop soon." And soon we reached a wooden shack. The leader of the group pushed the door open and announced, "We'll stay here tonight. There's a stove so you can fix yourselves something to eat."

We entered a small room with a ladder that went up to a loft. There was no furniture except for a few big boards and a charcoal pit in the center of the room that served as a stove. We put down our bags, grabbed some wood from outside, and built a fire. Its warmth felt like sheer luxury after the chilly nights we'd spent shivering in the bushes. We had some food that was hot for the first time in what felt like a year and by the time we were finished with our meal, the forest was pitch-black and we could hear animals howling within its depths. I shivered in spite of the heat from our fire and Lao Yang lit a cigarette to calm his nerves.

"What kind of animal is making that noise?" he asked, and the leader of the villagers said, "Who knows? We no longer have hunters in our village—they died out years ago. Only the men who are old and bedridden would know what beasts roam these forests; all we know is that they are dangerous and hungry animals. None of us men ever sleep more than half the night. We take turns staying awake to feed our campfire, keeping the wild things at bay and ensuring our safety."

I was too tired to care about anything the man had to say. "I'm taking the last watch," I told Lao Yang. "Wake me up when it's my turn." He started to bitch at me but I muttered, "Don't make me regret coming along to help you or I just might leave." And then I fell asleep, only to dream that I was still wide awake. Then suddenly I was awake; Lao Yang was shaking me and whispering, "Wake up, damn it. Get up right now!"

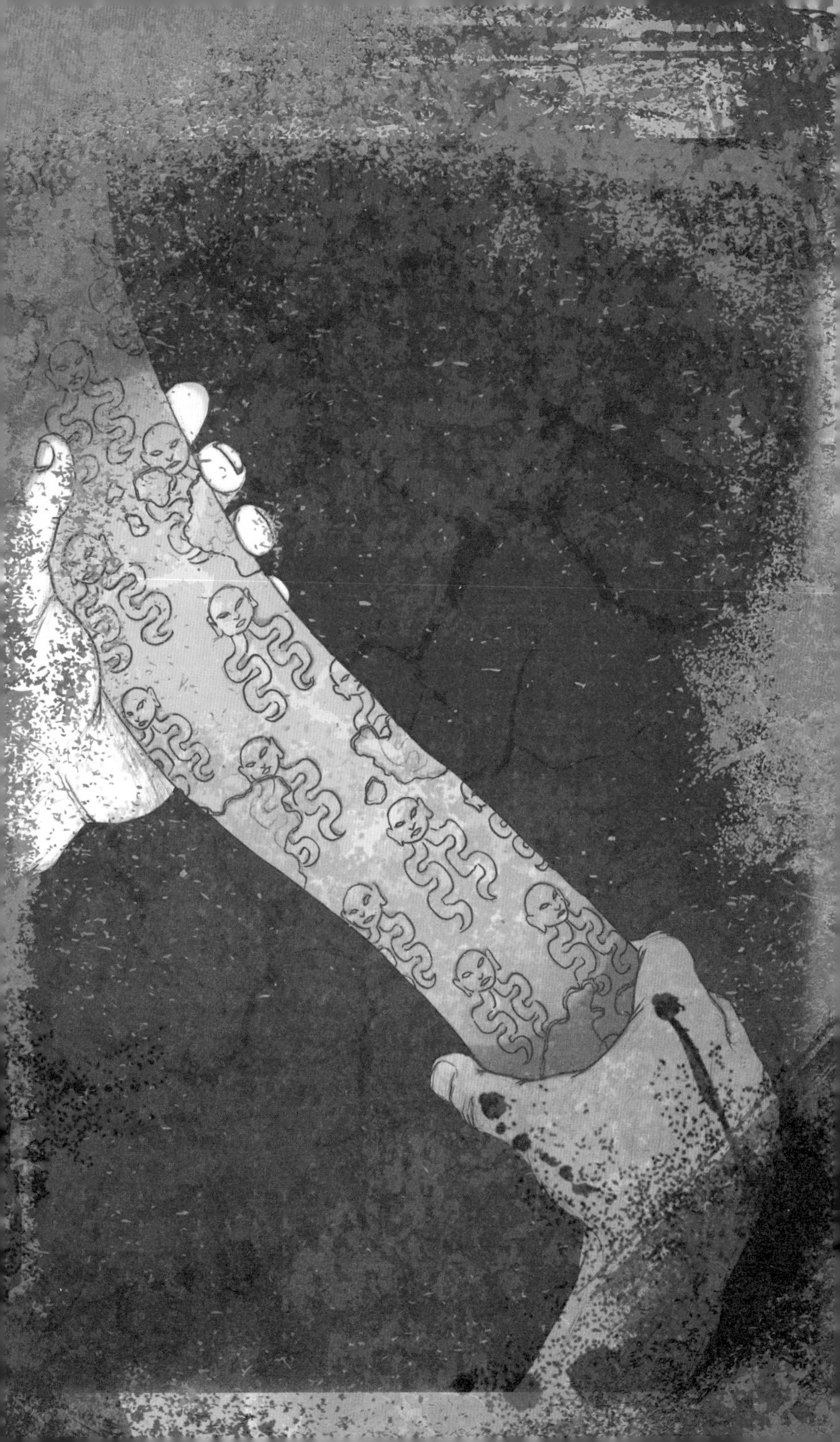

CHAPTER SEVEN

EXCAVATION

I was furious. I began to yell at Lao Yang for disturbing me but he put his hand over my mouth and hissed, "Don't say anything—just come with me."

"What's going on? What happened?"

"Follow me. I have something to show you."

He was dead serious so I crept out of the shack behind him. In front of us stretched the forest. Lao Yang took out a compass to determine our position. He had a folding shovel in his hands and two flashlights. He gave one to me and we followed in the direction of the night wind for about ten minutes. Then he plunged his shovel into the ground and said, "This is it."

"What the hell? Did we come out here to plant a tree?"

"Last time when I was with my cousin, we spent the night right here. I found him sneaking out in the middle of the night and didn't know what he was doing, so I followed him. It turned out that he was burying something right here, but our situation was pretty bad at that point so I didn't have time to think about it. I just wanted to get out of here as soon as possible, so I forgot about it. Now that I think of it, there was something weird about that night."

"Are you sure this is where he buried whatever it is?" I asked.

He nodded. "My cousin had been a little deranged after finding that bronze tree. I don't know what kind of black magic hit him but I'm sure he was hiding something from me. Now that we're here, let's dig and have a look at what he buried. You watch for anyone coming this way."

I nodded, and Lao Yang thrust down the shovel.

The site didn't seem hard to excavate, but the villagers were asleep not too far away, and we didn't want to wake them. So after every three shovels full of dirt, Lao Yang would stop so we could listen for anyone moving in our direction.

He dug for about a half hour until I began to wonder if he was mistaken about this being the right spot. Suddenly his shovel struck some sort of metal; he stopped digging, leaned over, and brought out something that looked like a stick.

It was covered with dirt and looked a lot like a bone. Lao Yang wiped away the dirt and said, "Shit. It's this?"

I leaned over to take a look and saw a long piece of bronze covered with green verdigris. There were cracks at the base where it had been cut with a special saw, and under the beam of the flashlight I could make out a pattern that looked like a serpent with two bodies joined by one head with a human face. It looked as though it came from the She Kingdom that my grandfather's old friend had told me about.

"Fuck this," Lao Yang exploded, "this is the bronze branch that I told you about. I can't believe my cousin secretly sawed it off the tree. What a bastard."

I frowned. People like that were the lowest of the low in

the world of grave robbers, and there were unfortunately quite a few. It was just another day's work for them to destroy a piece of art that would be the pride of any museum just so they could gain a few thousand dollars.

Lao Yang continued to dig but nothing else turned up. He refilled the hole with dirt, and we wrapped the bronze branch neatly in a piece of cloth and crept back into the shed. Everyone was still snoring but we were too excited to fall asleep again. Lao Yang sat across from me and began to add more wood to the bonfire.

He looked preoccupied again and I said, "You've been pretty manic-depressive these past few days. Do you have any other secrets you might want to reveal? Do you have hemorrhoids? A couple of children?"

He lit a cigarette and said, "It would be great if things were that simple. I just feel like there's something wrong—something I don't understand about my cousin. When I went into the mountains with him, he was normal. But once he saw that bronze branch, I felt like he began to get crazier and crazier."

"Do you think there's a connection between your cousin's madness and what you just dug up?"

Lao Yang nodded. "You can see for yourself, he secretly hacked off this branch and then he buried it. Does that make any sense to you?"

As I remembered the branch, I knew I'd seen something like it before. I remembered the book given to me by Mr. Qi, and its picture of the "Serpent Dragon Tree." Was it possible that the piece of bronze that Lao Yang had just dug up could be a tip of one of that tree's branches? If so, the tree could be hundreds of feet tall—a discovery that could shock the world.

I patted Lao Yang on the back. "Don't think too much. If it really was the branch that made your cousin go mad, by now you'd be as crazy as he is. You're as weird as hell but you aren't insane—so stop worrying, okay?"

CHAPTER EIGHT

INTO THE GORGE

After five hours of hard travel, we finally made it around Mount Serpent Head by the next afternoon. When we came to the first small village, we thanked the man who had helped us so much and went off on our own. Lao Yang had been here before and led me to the family he'd lodged with the last time.

The village was built on a steep side of the mountain and was filled with stone houses that had stood for several centuries. Its roads were paved entirely with quartzite all the way to the mountainside, and the foundation of a house at the highest end of the road was easily a hundred feet higher than one on the lowest end. Streams flowed through the roadside ditches and soft green moss covered every wall, constructed largely from bricks that had obviously come from ancient tombs.

We bought some food from our host family and took a bath in a nearby river. We washed our clothes, hung them to dry in the sunlight, and in our underwear, we sat at the bank of the stream, talking over the best way to proceed with our plans.

We knew by now we would never be able to catch up with our elusive gang of five. Our only hope was to find the mark

Lao Yang had made near the spot where he had found the bronze tree.

"What sort of mark did you make and why are you so positive you'll be able to find it now?

"When my cousin and I were here before, we passed through a very weird place that local people call the Gate to Hell. It has distinctive rock outcroppings and everybody around here knows about it. The burial pit isn't far from there but the gorge itself is more than twenty miles away from this village, at the edge of the thickest forest."

We no longer were so foolish as to think we could travel onward without a guide so we asked our friend, the village leader, if he could recommend someone trustworthy who could point us in the right direction.

The leader told his grandchildren to take us to the last of the old hunters and they led us to a white-bearded man who was sunning himself in front of a tile-roofed house. "There he is," the children told us. "That's Old Man Liu."

Old Man Liu hadn't been born in this village so people still thought of him as an outsider, even though he'd lived here since he was a young man. He was now over eighty but was still strong and healthy and a popular guide. We told him where we wanted to go and he shook his head. "Not a good idea. You can't go up to the Gate to Hell at this time of year."

"Why not?" I asked. "It's beautiful weather, clear sky, crisp air, best season for hunting. If we don't go there now, then when can we go?"

He told his son to get us some tea and said, "This season is an especially wicked time of the year in the mountains. This is when it's haunted. I'm more than eighty years old, and I'm not fucking with you. The Gate to Hell is actually a highway for the soldiers from the world of the dead. If you bump into them while they are marching on this route, you'll be swept along with them and your soul will never return."

There was no arguing with the man so we asked him to tell us the best route into the mountains.

"Go to the high mountain range near the Qin River and then walk to the west for seven days until you reach Mount Tianmen. There will be cliffs on either side of you at that point which are impossible to scale, but between the mountains is a strange opening just wide enough for two men walking side by side to pass through. This is known as a 'thread of sky,' or the Gate to Hell. According to an ancient legend, villagers once saw an army silently marching along the Qin River and into the 'thread of sky.' Once they walked into that opening, the earth began to tremble and shake; the entrance snapped shut, the troops were trapped within the mountain, and nobody ever saw them again.

"During the Qing dynasty a rich man sent a few Feng Shui masters to find the bodies of those soldiers. After spending ten days in the mountains, the masters returned so terrified that they were almost inhuman. They all said that there was a Waterfall of the Netherworld in Mount Tianmen. It was connected to the world of the dead; they had almost plunged over it to their own deaths, never to return.

"At first nobody believed them but then people began to say they heard galloping horses in the gorge and this rumor spread. Some people believed that soldiers from the world of the dead traveled through the Gate to Hell and the soldiers who had disappeared so long ago had actually been ghost soldiers returning to their home. You two can walk to Mount Tianmen—it will take about a week—but after that you should accept that this is as far as you will go. Nobody knows what waits in the forests beyond and nobody—not Tartar troops from the Qing dynasty nor the vanquished troops of the Kuomintang—who has gone there has ever returned. I won't take you there—nobody in this village will—but I'll give you directions on how to go alone. Remember, if you ignore my advice, I won't be responsible for what becomes of you."

My grandfather had mentioned in his journal that grave robbers need to pay attention to folklore so I respectfully listened to Old Man Liu and thanked him for his time.

He was a gentleman who probably didn't entertain many visitors anymore and was eager to tell us more stories. He was determined that we should be his guests for dinner, while we were determined to be on our way, so he wrapped up a meal for us to take along. The smell of roasted meat wafted from the packages and Lao Yang and I knew we wouldn't get far before tearing into our gifts.

We had a clear objective this time. Following our compass and pushing our bodies to their physical limits, we traveled over mountains and valleys and plunged into the most mysterious, vast, untouched forest in China's wilderness, a world so green and shadowy we felt as though we were walking underwater.

We trudged in dogged determination for a week. Lao Yang was the first to break our silence, yelling, "I can see the peak of Mount Tianmen through the treetops. Look!" Now that we were near our goal, we looked at each other and began to laugh.

"Shit, we need baths. In the state we're in there's no difference between us and the most isolated mountain savages," I said, and Lao Yang sniffed at his armpit, grimacing in agreement.

"Filthy or not, we've come to the right place," he told me. "After we make it through the Gate to Hell, we'll come to the pit that we've traveled so far to find—and then—well, you'll see."

I climbed up a towering cedar and took a peek through our telescope. Mount Tianmen loomed through the lens; its peak looked ghostly through the clouds that surrounded it, and the pine trees that were sprinkled on the slopes of the mountain were dark, making me think of the homes of demons. I could barely see the thin black line that marked the opening of the Gate to Hell, and when I finally caught sight of it, I felt a quick quiver of fear.

We got to the base of the mountain around noon and approached the rock-strewn entrance that marked the beginning of the Gate to Hell. It was a stunning sight, looking as though the mountain had been sliced with a sword, making a small crack through the rock face. That crevice was the pathway that had supposedly swallowed up soldiers centuries ago. The ditch was so narrow that only a sliver of daylight was visible at the top of its walls—as if the entire sky had been compressed into one thin line. This was the "thread of sky" that would lead us to safety or to our deaths.

The Gate to Hell was surprisingly beautiful, with hills and rock outcroppings sprouting from its floor like natural sculptures. Mountain streams sparkled near the edges of the pathway, making lovely bubbling sounds. The light that came from the "thread of sky" cast a bright golden glow on the walls of the crevice, making it look inviting and cheerful.

"As I remember, it took my cousin and me at least the whole afternoon to walk through this place," Lao Yang remarked. "We should eat something before we begin our hike."

We built a fire and ate the meat that the old hunter had given us. Now that we were near our goal, we gobbled it like pigs and when it was all gone, we realized we were still hungry. I reached to get more food from our bag but found it was gone. "Holy shit," I yelled, "our food bag has vanished."

"Damn you," Lao Yang shouted in reply. "Why did you spit the gristle from your meat down the back of my shirt?"

"What are you talking about? That meat was so damned good, I chewed every bit of it—why would I want to waste the gristle by spitting it at you, anyway?"

Lao Yang looked at me suspiciously, and I think he would have hit me if a bone hadn't fallen toward us from the top of the crack. Looking up, we saw a dozen big golden monkeys standing above us. The largest of them held our food bag and was slowly and methodically eating everything that was in it. When the bag was empty, the monkeys all looked at it as if they wondered how it might taste, but then they caught sight of our backpacks.

The biggest monkey, obviously the leader, swung over the edge of the trench and began to climb down toward us, followed closely by his gang. Obviously they thought we had more food and they were out to get it.

"We're in trouble now," I muttered. The leader of the monkey pack let out a screech of agreement as he and his group began to close in on us, baring their long, yellow fangs. They all growled as they approached, warning us to give them the bags without any trouble.

CHAPTER NINE

MONKEYS

Lao Yang and I each picked up pieces of blazing wood from our bonfire and brandished them at our attackers. The monkeys retreated, the slower ones with burned tails that we had ignited with our torches. But not all of the marauders fled. Some rushed unnoticed toward our backpacks and a small monkey snatched up a few waterproof bags that Lao Yang hadn't yet repacked. I rushed to recover the stolen belongings but another monkey took advantage of my defensive move and snatched my pack, dragging it off. It was too heavy for him to manage so he began to rummage through it in search of more portable items.

These monkeys were brilliant thieves; it was clear that we weren't the first humans they had robbed. Too bad we can't enlist them to help us with our grave robbing, I thought, and then yelled, "Fuck no!" as I saw the monkey pull a box of my favorite cookies from my pack. Racing toward it, I kicked the little brigand away from my food, picked up my precious cookies, and jammed them back into the safety of my pack.

Then a flash of yellow leaped in front of me—it was the monkey leader, its claws reaching for my face. I parried at it with my firewood torch but its claws raked across my hand, tearing it open in a long and bloody gash. I screamed and the firewood fell from my wounded hand.

The monkey rushed back in a second attack; I kicked at it as hard as I could but it clung to my leg, teeth buried in my calf. I could think of only one thing to do through the wave of pain that engulfed me and I bit the monkey on its face, feeling exultant when I drew blood. It turned to jump away from my assault; I reached blindly to grab at whatever was within my grasp and caught it by the tail.

A monkey's tail is crucial to its well-being and if it is caught during a fight, it means death for someone. The monkey leader roared and leaped toward my face but I turned sideways, swung it by its tail, and sent it hurtling toward the ground. If this didn't kill it, I was sure the force of the fall would at least make it lose consciousness.

But this monkey wasn't the leader for nothing. Not only did I fail to kill it, I didn't even hurt the damned thing. It screamed again and returned to the attack. Grabbing its tail once more, I threw it against a rock with all of my might. It rolled away, leaped back to its feet, and climbed to the top of a nearby hill, gibbering with pain.

I turned to check on Lao Yang and saw that he was in pursuit of the monkey that had stolen his waterproof bags. Since the gang saw that their leader had just been hurt, they fled to a safe distance, where they picked up stones to hurl at Lao Yang. The small monkey sat safely with the others, still clutching our bags.

These damned things had an advantage over us. It was their territory; they were lithe, agile, and talented at climbing; and they had no fear of humans. If they hadn't been terrified of fire, we'd be dead by now. And if two of them decided to attack one of us, we would be done for. I had no idea of what to do.

Lao Yang ran to my side, gasping for breath. "This is im—impossible. These monkeys are too quick. Let's get out of here now and just think of our lost possessions as an offering to the God of the Mountain."

There was no other solution. We had no way to prevail against these monkeys and if we tried, we'd probably only lose more of our supplies.

"Yes, you're right. There's a long road ahead of us and it's going to be rough walking it after dark. But take care of your stuff, damn it. Your carelessness cost us a lot of time."

"Okay, okay. I've got the point. It's in the past now, so stop talking about it, will you?"

We strapped our backpacks tightly to our chests and yelled at the monkeys to keep them from following us as we walked off down the narrow path. Bolting our way along the trail, we didn't take a breath until we were completely inside the Gate to Hell. The path became even narrower between the two mountain walls and we felt as though we were being pressed between them. Suddenly it was hard to breathe. It seemed as though the two sides of the mountain would become one solid rock before we came to the trail's end. Old Man Liu was right, I thought, this path really is the Gate to Hell. I remembered what he had said about the lost soldiers.

Lao Yang seemed to have the same thing on his mind. "You know," he said in a low voice, as though he was afraid to speak, "almost no one has passed through this crevice since it was first formed. But look, there are no weeds on the path, just as though horses' hooves stamped it clean every day."

We walked on and began to feel disoriented, even though there was only one path to follow. How much farther we would have to walk we had no idea, but we knew that the light was growing dimmer and the air began to hold a chill. It was frighteningly quiet within the mountain, except for the sound of the wind and some strange sounds that we couldn't identify.

"Do you feel as though we're being watched?" Lao Yang asked, and I nodded.

"I hope the monkeys aren't following us," he continued, and I shot him a furious glance.

"If you're going to babble on like that, then tell me a joke. Try to make me laugh, not scare the hell out of me."

He tried but it didn't work—I didn't laugh. All I could think about was that moment when the "thread of sky" overhead would disappear and leave us trapped in darkness. Lost in my imagination, I didn't notice that Lao Yang had stopped walking and I ran into his back with a jolt.

"You could have warned me that you stopped," I complained but grew silent when I saw his frightened face.

"There's a person—in—in front of us," he stuttered.

"What person? How is that possible? The nearest village is at least twenty miles away," I argued, but as I peered around Lao Yang's frozen body, I turned to ice myself. In the shadow of the wall ahead of us was the body of a man staring at us, his face hidden in shadow.

CHAPTER TEN

MAN OF STONE

Lao Yang and I simultaneously tried to step back in order to keep a distance from what we saw, but neither of us could move. Lao Yang was braver than I and managed to shout, "Who...who are you?"

There was no reply.

Lao Yang lowered his voice and asked, "Why is he ignoring us? Could this be one of the soldiers from the world of the dead that Old Man Liu told us about?"

A breeze wafted down through the trench and the fresh air it carried somehow cleared my mind. "Don't panic. Let's take a look first!" I took out my flashlight and pointed it at the figure.

The man was dressed in ancient clothing and his bare arms were grey. He stood woodenly in the middle of the Gate to Hell, looking extremely out of place in the dim shadows of the mountain. The beam of the flashlight was pointed directly at him, yet he didn't move or make a sound.

And then I noticed something truly bizarre.

Green moss was growing all over this man's body.

No living creature except a turtle would allow moss to sprout on its skin. As I looked more carefully, I realized this guy had no skin but was carved out of stone. It was so realistic that under the dim light, it was easy to think it was human.

And yet I couldn't laugh. The figure was sculpted with uncanny skill and was hideously lifelike, even as we drew closer to it. Who could have done this? And when? And why?

We forced ourselves to walk right up to the man of stone and found that below the waist it had been crushed in a fall, probably from the wall above. Part of its head had been destroyed as well. I looked up and saw a place above us that looked as though it might have crumbled.

Most intriguing to me was that double-bodied serpents were carved into his stone garments, which were clothes from a period I had never seen before. As I examined this figure, I was sure he was a burial object from a tomb, perhaps from the spot above us that had collapsed.

Lao Yang was already on his way up the slope and I followed close behind. We reached the spot we thought the statue might have fallen from and found a shallow pit dug near the edge of the cliff. Inside it were many statues like the one that had frightened us so badly. None of them had heads. Human skulls had been put on their necks, held in place with dried clay.

It looked as though once there had been murals covering the walls of the pit but rain had washed them all into solid blocks of color. Barely visible was the portion of a body carved on the cliff wall at the bottom of the pit. In the middle of the carving was a dark opening about as big as a basketball. I peered into the hole with my flashlight and discovered a huge cave inside.

This cave had to be an ancient tomb—I was sure of it. And it might well be related to Lao Yang's sacrificial pit that I'd heard so much about. But the hole in the carving made me certain that someone had already explored this burial site.

Whoever was able to build a tomb in this spot had to have been someone of high status. But whoever was able to rob a tomb in this spot, now he was a man to lavish with every respect. An ordinary grave robber, even if he walked through the Gate to Hell hundreds of times, would never think that above his head was another universe.

Lao Yang and I decided to go into the hole and take a look for ourselves. After all, our destination was nearby. If there was nothing inside, it wouldn't set us back too far, and it would be unforgivable for people in our line of work to pass up a cave without going in.

Lao Yang was thinner than I was so he was the first to enter. The position of the entrance was high above the cave itself; his feet couldn't touch the floor, so he stayed close to the wall as I handed him a flashlight. He took it and said, "Holy shit. There's a lot of water in here."

I stuck my head in and saw a large chamber with an arched ceiling that held traces of fading murals. There was a hell of a lot of water; it almost reached the ceiling. I could see shallow holes dug into the sides of the stone walls that were submerged in water. Headless statues covered with moss were everywhere I looked. I didn't know whether this water came from rain when it blew through the opening or if there was some other cause.

"The last time I was here," Lao Yang told me, "that body carved on the cliff wall was still in one piece. So this entry hole was made during the past three years."

It would have been impossible for rain to fill this huge cavern in such a short time, I realized, so why there was so much water here now was a mystery to me.

Lao Yang, confident in his swimming prowess, released his grip on the wall and jumped down into the water.

"Can you touch the bottom and tell if it's mud or stone?" I asked.

"I can't get to the bottom without diving," he replied. "Damn, this water is frigid. Can you see any icebergs floating around?"

I took our wetsuits from our backpacks, tossed his down to him, and put mine on. Then I gingerly eased my way into the water, which really did feel as though it came from a recently melted glacier.

Only emptiness lay beneath my feet. We paddled about, training our flashlights on the space before us and saw a stone door, wide open on the inside wall. Within the door was a dark tunnel that was the width of two army tanks. Its stone walls were a bluish grey color and held murals that were now so eroded that the pictures were almost invisible.

We swam down the tunnel for thirty feet until it suddenly bent into a ninety-degree angle. When I directed my flashlight into that new direction, I saw it went off into what looked like infinity. It would be stupid to go on, I thought.

Lao Yang glanced at the walls and asked me, "Have you noticed that even though this tomb is large, it was built rather badly? Look at these stone columns here. They look worse and worse as they go on, one after the other, unpolished and ugly. Perhaps the owner of this tomb wasn't very rich. Maybe he spent all his money on digging out the mountain and had nothing left to adorn the space."

"This could just be the outer edge of the entire mausoleum," I replied. "You see there are so many unfinished stone statues here. Maybe this is just where the workmen quarried and carved the rocks. Let's go in and take a look."

We swam for a few minutes past the turn and then heard splashes in the water ahead. It sounded as though something was moving underwater, coming closer and closer to us.

I jammed the flashlight into Lao Yang's hand so he could point it in the direction that the sounds were coming from. When he did, I could see a triangular mark appear on the surface of the water. Then it sank from sight.

Before I could react to what I had seen, Lao Yang pushed me, turned in the opposite direction, and yelled, "Swim for your life, damn it!"

CHAPTER ELEVEN

SALMON FROM HELL

My swimming skills were nowhere close to Lao Yang's. When I saw that triangular shape churn through the water as it rapidly came closer to me, I knew my only possible hope was fight, not flight.

Quickly I strapped my flashlight to my wrist, pulled out the hunting knife that was attached to my belt, and held my backpack in front of me to serve as a shield. "Help me!" I yelled to Lao Yang, but he had already dog-paddled at least thirty feet away.

"Fuck you and ten generations of your great-great-grandfathers," I howled. I ducked down and braced myself for a mighty blow from this thing that raced toward me. When it was three feet away, it disappeared and concentric circles appeared on the water's surface.

Then a blast of ripples appeared in front of me and a force like a cannonball crashed into my chest. Black water filled my mouth and nose; I was pushed into the water and shoved deep down.

I knew I was going to die; I had nothing to lose. I groped for my knife and began stabbing the water blindly. Something shook under my hand; I'd hit something but had no idea what it was. The creature that was trying to drown me twisted and lost its hold on me. I hurtled through the water and my head hit a wall.

But I was free. I struggled to get my head above water and gulped hard to fill my lungs with air. That damned thing nearly killed me, I thought, and looked about for that useless bastard Lao Yang.

All I could see was the beam of his flashlight behind me, casting a dim and reflective glow on the water.

As my lungs filled with oxygen, my mind became clearer and I realized my hunting knife was gone. Did I drop it or was it buried in the monster? Now I had no weapon and my backpack had been ripped to shreds, so I had no shield either. If that thing returned to have another go at me, he'd have an easy feast.

I had the impression that I'd been attacked by a giant fish but how could there be a fish in a sealed-off mountain cave, especially a mammoth monster like this? What the hell did it eat when I wasn't around for nourishment, rocks?

Lao Yang finally found me, shouting, "Are you okay? Didn't lose a shoulder or a leg, did you?"

"Stop," I yelled. "Don't come over here—that thing is still here somewhere."

"It should be fine. I was trying to make some noise just now to attract its attention. I thought—oh shit..."

A giant splash sent water shooting into the air and a fish the size of a baby elephant surfaced, pulling Lao Yang underwater.

I searched all over my body but found no weapons—only a sharp can opener. It was too short to be an effective knife but I'd have to make it work. I shouted, jumped into the water, and swam to where I'd last seen Lao Yang.

The water was ruffled by something moving under its surface; I began to grope about, hoping I'd touch Lao Yang. Before I could find anything, something that felt like a fish tail slapped me hard right in my face and for a second I was sure that my neck had snapped in two.

Furious, I pulled myself together and swam to where I was sure the fish would be. I caught hold of something smooth and scaly, raised my can opener, and began to stab at whatever was in my reach.

My improvised weapon cut through the fish easily and I swiped at it again and again. The water turned pink with blood. The fish tried to swim away from me, but I plunged the can opener even deeper and held onto it as though it were a harpoon. As the fish swam forward, the blade slipped along its flesh, opening a deep wound in its side, and the water went from pink to deep scarlet.

But the fish pulled away and then its head, mouth open and fangs bared, charged toward me once more. I tried to twist away but it threw itself upon me and pushed me deep underwater. There was nothing for me to grab, but a hand came out of the depths and pulled me to safety. It was Lao Yang, covered in blood and gasping for breath.

"Where did it bite you? Are you all right?" I babbled.

Grinning, he raised his backpack to where I could see it. Half of it was gone.

Nearby the water was roiling and we knew that damned fish had been badly injured by the can opener. It floated to the surface, belly up, fins wiggling weakly. Lao Yang and I both cheered but didn't dare to go near it until it was completely still.

It was at least six feet long, with a head the size of a

washbasin and a mouth full of small barbed teeth. A dagger protruded from its forehead; whether it was mine or Lao Yang's I couldn't tell. Some sort of weird pattern was visible on the top of its back. I'd seen pictures of this. It was a Siberian salmon, the most deadly of all fish, but how did it find its way into this cave?

"Come here," Lao Yang interrupted my thoughts, "look at this. There are stairs in this place."

During our struggle with the fish, we had entered the deepest part of the tunnel. Looking down into the cave, I saw simple, crude steps extending all the way to the edge of the water where the ground was raised. When I swept my flashlight into that area, I could see murals on the walls.

We were cold and hurt and longing for some rest. We agreed that what we needed was to get dry and do something about our wounds.

Lao Yang didn't say much. He lifted the fish by its gills and dragged it out of the water. "What do you want that thing for?" I asked and he replied, "It swallowed our equipment from our bags. How can I let that get away? We still need to use that stuff to make some money and I'm going to recover it all no matter what."

I shook my head but went up to help him carry the fish. The staircase we climbed was almost perfectly straight. Above us was a chamber supported by wooden columns that were thin and rotted. On one side was a tunnel that led to another room that was pitch-dark. The room above us was covered in murals, simply but abstractly drawn. In my present frame of mind, I was in no mood to admire them.

When we reached the upper room, we found some columns that had rotted through, used the wood to build a bonfire, and began to dry our saturated garments. "Now let's recover what was eaten," Lao Yang said. He slit open the fish's massive belly. "Look at how huge this thing is. I'm going to slice off some salmon steaks and see how it tastes."

I took some medicine from Lao Yang's torn backpack, cleaned my cuts, and wrapped them with bandages. "Enjoy your feast. I wouldn't eat anything that lived in this dirty water. Besides, I don't know where this fish came from, and what it ate to get that big. It's not very appetizing to think about."

Lao Yang had already dug into the fish's stomach and pierced its gallbladder with his knife. A stench filled the room, so terrible that I almost wished I were back with the monkeys again—anywhere but this place. I turned to look at what could smell so bad and saw that along with the pulpy mess that dripped from the fish's stomach, something round rolled out of it, moving in my direction and stopping in front of me. I took one look and nearly puked.

It was a human head.

CHAPTER TWELVE

THE HEAD

Trying hard to control my nausea, I flipped the head upside down with my knife and took a good look at it. Its face bore the marks of teeth, but the head itself was intact. When the fish had gulped down the head, it probably didn't bother to chew it very much.

Whoever this was, he hadn't been in the fish's stomach very long. Since the digestive process hadn't broken down the flesh on his skull, I knew he had just recently been devoured, probably not long before the fish turned his lethal attentions in our direction.

Covering my nose with one hand, I dabbled with my knife through the reeking fluid that dripped from the fish's stomach, looking for the body that went with the head. There was a hand and some chunks of flesh, all damaged by gastric juices.

As I continued my grisly search, I found the bags that the fish had swallowed, with their contents doused in partially digested food that had probably once been the body attached to the head. I decided we could do without all but the most essential supplies in these bags; although our food supplies were swaddled in plastic wrapping, I knew I would never be able to put any of it in my mouth knowing where it had been.

"Do you think somebody has a farm of carnivorous salmon in this tunnel?" Lao Yang asked.

"No, I think there are other water-filled tunnels in this area that connect to a subterranean stream that flows from the Jialing River. The salmon probably followed the stream and ended up here. And I hope there was only one of them who took the wrong turn."

We pushed the dead fish and the human head back into the water, but the stench lingered and it was truly intolerable. We put our clothes back on after they were almost completely dry, shoved everything that we needed back into our bags, and left rapidly, with Lao Yang in the lead.

We walked swiftly into the tunnel. The beams of our flashlights showed stone statues of men and animals, and the cracked walls were occasionally ornamented with bas-relief figures carved into the rock.

"I hope there's an exit at the end of this tunnel—and maybe a tomb entrance as long as I'm making wishes. And I wish my damned flashlight would stop flickering," Lao Yang complained.

"It's probably just the battery. Let's take a little rest while you put in a new one and I have a quick cigarette."

We sat on the ground as I lit my cigarette and the flare of my lighter illuminated the lifelike stone figures that surrounded us.

"These statues are carved so well they almost frighten me," Lao Yang remarked. "What dynasty do you think they came from? I don't have a clue."

"Neither do I," I admitted. Chinese sculpture has a long history, with influences from ancient Indian and Tibetan cultures. As far as I knew, realistic carving techniques were used only once, when the terra-cotta warriors and horses of the First Emperor were made. These statues were completely lifelike as well, with the pattern of the double-bodied serpent adorning their bodies. Whether or not this cave was part of the ancient tomb that we searched for, there was no doubt that we were now in what had once been the territory of the She, that ancient serpent kingdom.

After Lao Yang replaced his battery, his flashlight revealed that we were at the tunnel's end. There was a stone wall in front of us and a room full of headless statues, surrounded by stone lamps.

In the middle of the chamber was a huge stone coffin placed on a platform, with nothing else near it. A double-bodied serpent was beautifully carved on its partially opened cover. The two bodies of the snake twined around both sides of the coffin, but its tail had never been carved. Only a vague outline showed where it was meant to be.

Lao Yang and I peered about and finally came to the side of the coffin. Lao Yang had never seen one before; he walked around it twice and asked, "Could there be a zombie inside?"

"No. I've never heard of someone being placed into a coffin before it was completely carved. This has to be empty."

Lao Yang pointed his flashlight into the partially opened cover and peered through the crack. "But it looks like there's something inside. Come take a look if you don't believe me."

I walked over and looked. Through the crack I could see a black shadow lying inside.

"Should we open the cover and see what's inside?" he asked.

I was feeling a little unsure of myself. Before when coffins had been opened, there were a lot of experienced grave robbers around; this time I was the only one.

I shook my head. "There's something wrong. I don't feel good about this coffin. Don't be in a rush to open it."

Suddenly Lao Yang pulled back his hand, stepped away from the coffin, and fell flat on his butt.

"What the hell..." I began, but a cold grip engulfed my own hand and I looked down to find pale, twiglike fingers reaching from the coffin and clutching my wrist.

CHAPTER THIRTEEN

UNDERGROUND RIVER

I tried not to scream, tugging my hand from the one that was doing its best to drag me into the coffin. I reached for a gun but before I could take aim and fire, I heard something behind me. My hand that held the gun was pulled behind my back; I yelled as I began to struggle against this new attack.

Somehow I broke free of the hand from the coffin but then I tripped and fell, rolling on the ground. I leaped to my feet, ready to shoot whoever had grabbed me from behind—for some reason, I was sure it was a human.

I heard an explosive sound, something struck me on the head, and I dropped to the ground once more. Two people grabbed me by the arms, raised me to my feet, and pulled me over to the coffin. They had already captured Lao Yang, who was tied up and flat on his back. I was soon beside him, my hands tied behind my back with my belt.

Only then did I see the faces of our assailants. They were the five men we followed and then lost track of—Uncle Tai, Pockmark, and the rest.

How did they get here? Had they done what Lao Yang had suspected they might, turned the tables on us and followed us after we lost track of them?

Never before did I ever feel so frightened. There was nothing to keep these guys from killing us, and in this place, our bodies would never be found.

But once they tied us up, the men ignored us and went straight to the coffin. Lao Yang and I saw the ghostly hand still hanging over the edge of the cover and I yelled, "What are you doing? There's a zombie in there! Once you release it, it will kill us all."

They stopped, but only because they were laughing too hard to move. One of them said, "What zombie? Take a good look at what's inside!"

Then he pushed the coffin cover open and a skinny old man rose up from inside. He looked familiar and then I realized it was Uncle Tai. Damn it, we were tricked, I thought.

The old bastard stood up and put his pale, corpselike hand into his pocket. He jumped out of the coffin and walked over to where Lao Yang and I lay on the ground. He waved his hand at us and I noticed that his fingernails were long, sharp, yellow claws.

Uncle Tai stared at us silently and then lit a cigarette as he spoke to his companions. Since he used their dialect, I couldn't make out a word of what he said but I was sure they were planning how they were going to dispose of us. However, their attention was still focused on the coffin.

Switching to Mandarin, Uncle Tai said, "Mr. Wang. According to the position of the Eight Diagrams in Chinese mythology, Mr. Lee was certain that this must be the entrance to the underground waterways of the mausoleum. But there's nothing here. What's up?"

A fat, middle-aged man bent down with great effort. He

took a notebook from a bag, scanned it quickly, and said, "He's right. This is the place. The entrance was probably hidden when the tomb was sealed. There ought to be a trapdoor somewhere in this room."

Uncle Tai looked around and asked another person, "Liang. You're an expert in these matters. What do you think?"

The person he spoke to was sitting in the dark and I couldn't see his face. "I've looked at Mr. Lee's map and I'm sure it's accurate. I poked around here just now and if there is a trapdoor, it has to be on the platform underneath the coffin."

They lowered their heads and examined the area under the coffin; Old Tai knocked on it with the handle of his pistol. "How do you open it?"

Liang thought for a while. "I don't know. Push against it and see what happens."

Uncle Tai stood up and walked over to the young man. The two of them propped their shoulders against the coffin and pushed. Their faces turned scarlet and they grunted heavily but their efforts paid off. There was a clicking sound, the coffin moved slightly, and a black gap appeared in the burial platform.

The others went over to help and pushed hard against the heavy stone coffin, finally moving half of it away from its resting place. There was an entrance three feet wide.

I craned my neck to take a look. It was dark inside but I thought I could see a very steep staircase leading down from the entrance. Pockmark pointed his flashlight into the opening. He started to stick his head in to take a look, but was stopped by Uncle Tai. The older man pointed to me with his chin; Pockmark nodded, came over, and pulled me to the side of the cave. He loosened the bonds on my hands and my feet, then pushed me to the opening, pointing his gun at my head and gesturing for me to go in first.

So this is what they have planned for us, I realized. We're going to be their guinea pigs; if there were traps or other dangers, we'd serve as a warning to them. Why the fuck did I ever agree to come with that asshole Lao Yang? I knew what was probably waiting for us in this tomb—deathtraps, corpse-eating insects, homicidal plants, zombies—the list was endless. We were going to die.

I might as well turn and fight since I'm going to die anyway, I thought. At least if I resisted them, I had a slim chance of surviving. But Lao Yang caught my eye and whispered, "It's safe. You'll be okay. Go into the cave."

How the hell did he know that? He'd never been here before and so far he'd shown no knowledge that I didn't already have myself. But judging by the expression on his face, he seemed to think he knew what he was talking about. I tied my flashlight to my wrist, put both hands firmly on the wall of the opening, and lowered my body into the cave.

I took a deep breath and pointed my flashlight into the blackness. The staircase was almost perfectly straight and so deep I couldn't see the end of it. The green stone walls on four sides for some reason were very wet, too slippery to hold onto. Yet there was no water under my feet so I had no idea where the moisture came from.

I kept staring into the dark. Uncle Tai tapped my head and handed me a whistle. He said, "When you get to the bottom, blow this whistle. If we don't hear you in half an hour, we'll kill your buddy."

Where did the old jerk think I was going to run off to, anyway? I took the whistle and scrunched down into the tunnel.

It was hard work climbing down the steep, straight steps. Whoever built them weren't master craftsmen; some of the steps were terribly narrow and I could only put half of my foot on many of them. My toes began to cramp and it was hard to breathe. I looked up; the door above me was a small square of light in a world of blackness. A few shadows occasionally blocked out part of the light; my progress was being monitored.

At first, I was worried that there might be traps installed in this staircase, so I moved cautiously and slowly. Then I realized whoever was responsible for the poor workmanship of this place certainly didn't have the skill to place an effective trap.

As I continued my descent, the tunnel took on a gradual angle and the stairs became less of a problem. I noticed that the rock on the walls of this section had changed from dark green to a reddish brown color. Light bounced back at me when the beam of my flashlight hit the wall.

This rock was probably granite, with specks of reflective mica gleaming in its surface. Granite would mean I was now inside the mountain.

I began to hear the sound of moving water and the farther I went, the louder it became. It sounded like a full-size river with a rapid current.

I looked at my watch. I'd been gone for nearly twenty minutes and was afraid if I kept going, the sound of a whistle might not make it back up to the tunnel's entrance. I blew several times, hoping for Lao Yang's sake that our captors would hear me. The sound was soon echoed by a responding whistle from above and I felt a surge of relief.

I discovered the tunnel became wider as I went farther into it; I could see an opening ahead of me. A strong wind rushed through it, carrying a blast of fresh air. I ran a few steps forward, and suddenly I heard a roaring sound; I had come out of the tunnel and was on the banks of a huge river that was about as wide as a basketball court, flowing through a cave that was easily thirty feet high. I could see no end to it either on the left or the right. It was impossible to tell whether it was a natural cavern or if it were man-made.

The river was incredibly swift and the thunderous sound it made was enhanced by the acoustics of the cavern it flowed through. I waded into it and felt my feet begin to burn; in seconds I was in scalding hot water up to my knees. I got out fast.

I looked around and saw the banks of the river grew closer together and the river became narrower a bit farther into the cave. On the cave wall near the left bank hung many chains, and I tried to think of why they might be there. Somehow they didn't look reassuring.

As I pondered what I saw, Pockmark emerged from the tunnel and plunged into the river. He leaped back out in a second, yelling, "Damn, that water is hot enough to cook me."

Another young man followed close behind the first. This guy wore glasses and looked very intellectual. He had to be Liang. As he got closer, I discovered he wasn't as young as he looked from a distance; he was easily middle-aged.

The third person who came out was Lao Yang, followed

by that fat, middle-aged guy, Mr. Wang. Then came Uncle Tai. Where's Mr. Lee? I wondered. He was the one who had seemed to be in charge when we spied on them a few nights ago.

They all turned on their flashlights and several beams swept back and forth. Liang exclaimed in a low voice, "This is incredible. The path leading to the mausoleum is actually an underground river. If I didn't see this for myself, I'd never believe it."

Pockmark took a few steps forward in the water, yelped, and came back. He said to the others, "It's as deep as it is scalding. Uncle Tai, it's going to be tough getting through this place."

Uncle Tai looked at Mr. Wang and asked, "Where do we go from here? Does it tell you on your treasure map?"

Mr. Wang flipped through his book and said, "It says on the map that the last time the deaf-mute troop came here, they placed two metal chains underwater. If you walk along holding the chains, you'll arrive at the entrance of the underground tomb."

They all pointed their flashlights into the water. Sure enough a black metal chain as thick as a man's wrist lay at the bottom of the river. Uncle Tai pulled part of it out of the water, weighed it in his hand, and said, "Damn, this is heavy."

Pockmark went over and tried to pull it up to the surface a few times. "Uncle Tai, we can't do this. Mr. Lee just died a terrible death. If we come across that kind of fish again, we'll die too."

Liang quickly put a finger in the river and just as quickly pulled it back out. "Don't worry. There must be a hot spring somewhere on the riverbed. There can't be any fish here—they'd all be cooked."

He opened his mouth to continue his speech when a huge blast of water struck us all on the back. Its force sent us into the river; I looked back to see a geyser shooting from within the river up to the roof of the cave. Boiling water fell around us like raindrops and Uncle Tai stood up, gun in hand, yelling, "What the hell is going on here? And where's my nephew?"

CHAPTER FOURTEEN

WATERFALL

Pockmark had been tossed into the air when the geyser hit and was gone without a trace. The column of water continued to spout ferociously, as though it were being blown sky-high by a mammoth whale. Or maybe, I thought in a state of near delirium, it was caused by a sixty-foot version of our killer salmon who'd managed to swim through this river without being cooked.

A head bobbed up from the water and Pockmark pulled himself up onto the bank, his body bright red and severely blistered. He seemed to be blind; he stumbled back toward the edge of the river, fell in again, and floated upon the surface, unmoving.

Enraged, Uncle Tai kicked me in the ribs and yelled, "Get my nephew, you useless piece of shit." I could feel his gun poking a hole in my back so I plunged into the river.

Sprinkles of boiling water from the geyser ricocheted down from the cavern's roof and as they rained down on me, blisters formed when they hit my body. I grabbed Pockmark. His body was as hot as a glowing poker and I released him immediately. There was no point in rescuing this guy—he was cooked meat.

Another explosion tore through the air, and from the

top of the geyser came a plume of yellow vapor, smelling like a mixture of gas and sulphur. No fish could have caused this; it had to have come straight up from hell.

Lao Yang shouted, "Why are you frozen there? Quick—dive under the water before you become an ingredient in this devil's soup!"

The geyser was growing larger; it showered off the cave's ceiling in a deadly downpour. Its drops landed on the riverbank, and Lao Yang and our captors rushed to follow me as I dove below the surface of the river.

The scalding water from the geyser quickly permeated the river, and even well below the surface, the temperature was hot enough to hard-boil an egg. I swam underwater for a few minutes, then came back up to the surface for a quick look. Steam was rising from the river as far as I could see and I realized if we didn't find a safe place on dry land quickly, we'd soon be as well cooked as Pockmark.

It was impossible to go back to the tunnel we had used as our entrance to this damned place. Bubbles were forming on the water at that spot; the river there was coming to a boil. We had to keep going and swim as fast as we could to outrace the output of the geyser. "Follow me," I yelled to Lao Yang as I increased my speed, passed Uncle Tai and the others, and took the lead.

Caught up in the swift current, I let myself float and soon realized the water was becoming cooler. I turned to reassure Lao Yang but he looked far from comforted. "Stop! Stop! Watch out!"

Something crashed into him and pushed his head underwater. I could hear a roaring sound and looked ahead. Water splashed and rolled over a precipice inches away from me and a thunderous noise rose up toward me. "Shit," I yelled, "what kind of waterfall is this anyway?"

Lao Yang's head rose out of the river and he shrieked, "Get over to the side of the current and stay there or you'll be dashed to pieces."

I did as he told me and got as close to the cavern wall as I could. Clinging to a rock outcropping, I was jolted from safety as Liang crashed into me full force, sending both of us into the middle of the raging current and near the edge of the waterfall. I reached out instinctively and my fingers closed over the links of an iron chain.

It was taut and secure within the insanity of the rushing water and I clung to it as the rest of my body went over the edge of the precipice. I was suddenly swinging in midair, surrounded by the sound of cascading torrents of water and total blackness. My fingers tightened their grip.

Something pushed at my dangling legs; I looked and saw Liang clinging to another chain, with my feet resting on his head. I kicked at him savagely, stretched out one arm, and discovered a large number of underwater chains nearby, like a fence between us and the plunge of the waterfall. Many of them were broken, making wide gaps in the protective barrier.

Lao Yang floated toward me and I grabbed his arm, pulling him to safety. Uncle Tai and his fat boss grabbed at the chains nearby as the water bore them to our area. Pockmark's corpse became caught between two chains, and Lao Yang pulled a gun from the dead man's waistband. He aimed it at Uncle Tai and I pushed his arm down rapidly.

"What the hell are you doing? There's water in the barrel of that thing. Do you want it to backfire and kill you instead?"

Lao Yang shouted, "If we don't kill them now, we won't have another chance."

"You dumb fuck. Look behind you and see what's coming for us."

Steam rushed at our backs—the geyser had almost caught up with us and its heat rolled toward us like a tidal wave. I clamped my teeth together so hard that one of my molars shattered in my mouth. The only way we could survive was to surrender to the waterfall—and that might kill us as well. But it won't cook us, I told myself, and there's a chance we might survive our plunge into nothingness.

Liang, still clinging to the chain below me, yelled, "I have an idea! Pull me up and I'll tell you. If you don't, we'll all die together!"

I reached down, pulled him up, grabbed him by the throat, and shouted, "Tell us or I'll let you fall."

He glanced down at the raging water. Swallowing hard, he said, "Hot water floats on top of cold water. We'll dive down below the surface and wait for the boiling water above to float past us. If we can hold our breath while this happens, we'll survive."

We had no choice. I dove down into the water, hoping Lao Yang would have the brains to follow me. Grabbing onto a chain, I worked myself down toward the bottom of the river.

After going down about six feet, I could feel the water temperature begin to cool off. This just might work, I told myself, and concentrated every thought and muscle I had on holding my breath.

As I pulled myself down a bit farther on the chain, I felt my hand touch something solid and a face loomed toward me through the water. Protruding eyes bulged at me from rotting flesh and I gasped, choking on a mouthful of the river.

A corpse floated inches away from me, attached to one of the chains. Its tattered clothing was quite clearly winter gear and it was still carrying a backpack.

How did this guy get into this place and how did he die? I dug into his backpack; inside were some paints and an easel. Here was one of the art students who had disappeared—the old guy from the village had told us about them, I remembered dimly.

Bad luck for this boy, good luck for me. I needed a backpack since the salmon had demolished mine. As I robbed the corpse, I felt the water around me get warmer. The geyser had reached us; I plunged deeper into the river.

Liang was wrong. No matter how far down I went, the heat continued to follow. My skin began to throb and Lao Yang swam toward me, swinging his arms in pain. He kicked me hard and pointed toward the waterfall. We had the same idea; we had to go over the edge or be boiled alive like lobsters.

I glanced over at the corpse whose backpack I now carried and thought, I hope I'm not on my way to join you, little brother. I let go of the chain and let the current carry me over the cliff and into the spray of water.

14. WATERFALL

CHAPTER FIFTEEN

INTO THE POOL

I opened my eyes. I was in total darkness, lying on something flat and chilly. Off to the side I could hear running water. I had no idea of where I was or how I got here.

Memories began to return in fragments—the waterfall, the scalding geyser, the corpse with the backpack, the plunge into the abyss with Lao Yang beside me.

I raised my head and it struck something hard. Reaching up, I felt something like a plank, inches over my head. Had the waterfall washed me under some low-hanging rocks?

I groped further; all around me were rough wooden boards. I was enclosed in a space so small I could barely turn over. It was impossible for me to raise my head or my arms and legs more than a few inches.

I pushed on the boards above me and was amazed when they moved. Another push revealed a ray of light in the darkness. I knelt, carefully removed the boards, and sat up. "I'll be damned," I said, and my voice echoed around me.

I was sitting in a coffin, with the cover pushed to one side. Surrounding me was a room made completely of white Han marble, with a blazing torch in each corner. I looked up at the ceiling and saw it was covered by a painting of two intertwined pythons. It all looked very familiar to me but how did I get here? Who had put me in the coffin? And where the hell was Lao Yang anyway? We'd both plunged into the waterfall together—why wasn't he with me now?

I climbed out into the room and realized this place seemed to be almost an exact replica of the burial chamber in the undersea tomb where my Uncle Three had disappeared. Impossible, I thought—and then I realized someone had changed my clothes. I was now wearing a rubber wetsuit, the kind that divers used to wear in the '80s.

Grabbing a torch from one of the corners, I walked out of a doorway into a corridor made of white marble that led straight down to three doorways at the end of the hall. I'm out of my mind, I thought, this is exactly the same setup as that goddamned undersea tomb that I never wanted to see again.

What was going on? How did I get here? Was this a chamber very much like the one in the undersea tomb, or had I never come out of the undersea tomb at all?

I shook my head hard, raised the torch, and carefully looked around me for some sort of clue that would tell me where I was.

There was a wooden platform near the ceiling of the corridor, a bridge that would allow me to walk down the hallway without setting off any traps. Cautiously I climbed up onto it and walked to the end of the corridor. Light gleamed through the middle door but the other two were both completely dark.

I walked toward the door that the light came from and as I drew closer, I heard noises coming from inside the room. I pressed my ear to the door and I heard a cough, then a voice asking, "What should we do now? Should we open the coffin or not?"

Another voice, sounding very tentative, replied, "Sansheng said not to touch anything; let's do as he says."

I knew I had to be crazy now—that first voice was somebody who absolutely could not be here—it was good old Poker-face, Zhang Qilin. I had no idea who the other guy was but the name he mentioned belonged to my Uncle Three. What the fuck—how could Uncle Three be here?

But there were more surprises—a third person said, "Sansheng is still sleeping. We're only opening it to take a look. What's the difference? I'm on Zhang Qilin's side."

That third voice belonged to a woman.

What were they talking about? Qilin wanted to open a coffin but another guy was indecisive because of Uncle Three's warning. And a woman spoke up to support Qilin. What was going on? Could Qilin somehow have found Uncle Three?

As I continued to try to figure out this puzzle, I crawled to peek through the crack in the door to see the speakers. My view was limited; I could only see the back of a woman dressed in a wetsuit in the same color as mine. She was very tiny with braided hair; she looked almost like a child.

A fourth voice spoke up, "What happened to Qi Yu? That kid is a real pain in the ass. Where is that jerk? We can't just leave him here."

I froze. Qi Yu. He had been one of Uncle Three's comrades when the underground tomb was first discovered twenty years ago. Then the woman moved away and I could see Qilin standing beside a black coffin.

Another woman walked toward him and when her face came into sight, I almost screamed. I had seen her before—or at least her photograph. She was Uncle Three's lost love and a woman who had claimed my own imagination. This was Wen-Jin, exactly as she looked in photographs from decades earlier, when I was still a little boy.

Still another man whom I couldn't see said, "We'll never find Qi Yu. This undersea tomb is too huge. I say let's forget about him. We'll blaze a trail that he can follow, if he's still alive. Open the coffin, Zhang Qilin."

Suddenly sounds of roaring water came from the doorway on the left. "What's that? Let's go and find out," Qilin said and ran toward the door. I had just enough time to hide myself behind the door to the right, quickly extinguishing my torch, before people streamed out from the middle chamber. As they ran through the door on the left, I heard a woman exclaim, "Come and see—there's a pool here, look!"

I had heard all of this before—Zhang Qilin had told me this story when we were in the undersea tomb. It was what had happened long ago on the expedition when Uncle Three fell asleep and Wen-Jin vanished forever. How could I be reliving this? Was I hallucinating or had I gone thoroughly nuts?

Once again I was in the dark, both mentally and physically. I almost switched my flashlight back on when I saw a light approaching. The person holding it came down the same bridge near the ceiling that I had followed. He reached the door on the left, hid himself behind it, and frowned, looking very upset.

Now I knew I was insane. The man I was looking at was

my Uncle Three, looking the way I remembered him from the days of my childhood.

When the voices of Zhang Qilin and the rest of the group faded away into the distance, I realized they had probably gone down the pool's spiral staircase. My uncle switched off his flashlight and slipped through the door of the left-hand chamber. No matter if this is a hallucination or a dream, I still have to follow him, I thought.

I had just reached the left-hand door when my uncle popped back out, grabbed me by the throat, and whispered, "Following me, are you?" His fingers tightened and I knew he was going to strangle me.

I tried to cry out, "Uncle Three! I'm your nephew!" My words couldn't get past his encircled fingers and I struggled to break his grip, twisting desperately.

"For God's sake, wake up. Are you having a nightmare?"

Uncle Three dissolved into the darkness and Lao Yang was there instead, shaking me out of a haze. I touched my neck and sat up.

Lao Yang and I were on a rocky beach, with a pool nearby. The sounds of the waterfall were in the distance but I couldn't see it. A campfire blazed cheerfully beside us and Lao Yang moved me closer to it as I shivered.

"Are you okay?" he asked.

I waved my hand and smiled, bewildered by my vivid dream. Why, I wondered, could I still feel the grip of my uncle's fingers on my throat?

Lao Yang handed me a flask of water. I took a sip and asked in a hoarse voice, "Where are we? What happened to us?"

"This is the edge of the pool underneath the waterfall.

The waterfall is just over there. After we fell, you passed out and I had to drag you to safety so you wouldn't be pulled back in. You really should thank me—it almost killed me."

"Thanks," I muttered and then cursed as I tried to stand up. Every muscle felt bruised but I didn't seem to be injured anywhere. I forced myself to take a few steps and looked around.

The beach we were on was small and crescent shaped, bordering a gigantic, dark pool. We were in a large cavern; stalactites as thick as my legs hung from its ceiling, forming eerie columns under the flickering light of our campfire.

We were the only people on the beach. I asked Lao Yang, "What happened to Uncle Tai and the other guys?"

"I'm afraid those sons of bitches weren't as lucky as we are. I didn't see them after we leaped into the waterfall so I don't know if they were with us or not. I guess if they followed us, they were either washed to a different spot or maybe they drowned." He paused and then continued, "But our situation isn't exactly ideal; we lost all our equipment and I'm lost as well. You see how many tunnels are in the walls around the pool? It's like a maze. Damned if I know which way to go."

I began to count. There were at least seven or eight tunnels above the pool's water level that were large enough for us to stand up in and probably more in the darkness beyond the light of our fire.

"According to that fat jerk from Guangdong, we need to find the submerged chain that was used to lead people out of this cave in ancient times. It ought to be somewhere in this pool, leading to the end of a secret tunnel. If we can find it, it will take us to the heart of the ancient tomb."

Lao Yang frowned and replied, "Speaking of chains, I just remembered something. You know, I was conscious all throughout our fall. We were about twenty or thirty feet deep when we hit the bottom and all around us were those stone statues we saw in the cave when we came in. And I'm pretty sure I caught a quick glimpse of a chain lying at the bottom of the pool. But it didn't lead into a tunnel—it went straight into that crashing water coming down from the fall."

"How the hell is that possible? Is the tunnel beyond the waterfall, hidden in the rapids?"

I thought for a minute or two and then everything fell into place. "I get it now," I said. "The tomb we're looking for isn't part of our living world. It's hidden in the world of the dead."

"What sort of bullshit are you trying to feed me? We're not in a fucking ghost story, you know."

"Remember the Waterfall of the Netherworld and the legend of the dead soldiers that Old Man Liu told us about? Think about the waterfall we just survived. Because of the yellow gas in the hot water geyser, the waterfall is a weird saffron color, one that in ancient times was considered a hue found in the world of the spirits. So people decided the falls were part of the world of the dead and named the waterfall accordingly."

"It may look that way but it's not a credible theory. Only people who have been inside the mountain and followed the tunnel inside would know about the waterfall." Lao Yang stopped and then blurted out, "Oh shit, the guy who invented the legend of the soldiers was a grave robber too, wasn't he? Of course he wanted to frighten people away from this place."

"Congratulations, my boy—at last you show a tiny shred of logical reasoning in that thick head of yours. Now keep thinking. If the chain passes through the waterfall, then it would lead to the tunnel that is the passage to the tomb. So it could be said that the tomb could be found in another world—perhaps the spirit world, maybe even hell itself."

"Don't try to scare me. If we're going to enter the spirit world, don't we have to be dead to get inside?"

"You superstitious idiot, remember this legend was created by grave robbers to protect their territory. There are two explanations here—one is that this was a sort of secret code for what is a passageway between an ancient tomb and the world of the present day. The second explanation is that someone saw something in the passageway that made them feel as though they had entered the world of the dead. If that's the case, then we have to prepare ourselves for something horrible on our way to the tomb."

Lao Yang was dead silent after he heard this and finally muttered, "I say we forget about this and turn back while we can."

I shook my head. "We got here by the skin of our teeth. What a waste of time and energy if we didn't keep going—and even if we did turn around, how do you suppose we'd make it back up that damned waterfall? Our only choice is to get to the tomb and then find our way out from there."

Lao Yang shrugged. "Whatever you say. Let's check our

equipment and see what's left."

We still had one old sawed-off shotgun and the pistol Lao Yang took from Pockmark's body; in the backpack I had taken from the corpse of the art student there was some canned food, water, and even a jug of wine, along with a few pairs of gloves, pencils, and jars of oil paint.

"Useless crap," Lao Yang grumbled and began to toss it into the fire. "Wait," I said, "this stuff might be useful—let's take it all."

Our biggest problem was we no longer had our flashlights. Mine was long gone and the battery in Lao Yang's was stone dead. And we could hardly carry flaming torches with us into the waterfall.

"There's only one solution," Lao Yang decided. "Gather all the wood we can find here on the beach and make one hell of a huge fire. Its light will illuminate what we're getting into and will guide us back if we decide we need to do that."

"Okay," I agreed, "let's go."

We took off our clothes and stuffed them into the bag. Then we used the gloves and some sticks to make several short torches. We put them in the waterproof compartment of the backpack and built up the fire until its flames soared high above our heads. We warmed ourselves until we could no longer bear the heat, then jumped into the pool and began to swim toward the roar of the waterfall.

The water was brutally cold. The noise from the waterfall grew louder and we stopped, treading water as we decided which direction we should take before moving further.

"Do you see that?" Lao Yang shouted as something darted across the water not far from us. He pulled his pistol from his pack and raised it as he scanned the water. "It couldn't be another one of those fucking salmon, could it?" he asked.

"If it was, we'd be dead by now. Just keep going. Once we get to the tunnel, we'll be safe from whatever it is." There was a loud splash nearby and the two of us resumed swimming, but much more quickly than before. The water current was swifter by the second and we knew we were coming close to the falls. I was stiff with cold and Lao Yang was slowing down as well. We plowed through the water but our energy was almost gone.

"This isn't going to work," Lao Yang yelled. "The water's becoming too turbulent. Get as close to the bottom of the pool as you can and try to ride the current to get to the other side of the waterfall."

He dove beneath the surface and I followed, swimming to the bottom of the pool. In front of us, on the bed of the pool, was a fuzzy white light beaming through the water. Holy shit, I thought, it's my expensive high-tech waterproof flashlight, worth every yuan I spent on it. I gathered my remaining strength and swam toward it.

In the beam of light I could see many of the statues Lao Yang had mentioned, along with a stone platform with something shaped like a body shrouded in white floating on top of it. But all I cared about at this moment was the incredible, miraculous reappearance of my flashlight.

As I inched my way toward it, holding on to the closest stone figures for support, a surge of water struck my back with stunning force. A large white shape loomed ahead of me and hit my hand hard. I lost my grip on the statue and my body began to float back up to the water's turbulent surface. Whatever had hit me had moved off to the side as the water whirled me about like a piece of driftwood.

I'm dead now, I thought, and could feel myself begin to blur into unconsciousness. Then my back hit something hard and the pain woke me up. I grabbed at what I had banged into—it was a chain stretched tightly through the water. Lao Yang had been right; maybe we might make it out of this damned place alive after all.

CHAPTER SIXTEEN

ONE OF THE GANG

Suddenly I didn't care about my flashlight or whatever had kept me from recovering it. I pulled myself down along the chain, coming close to the spot under the waterfall. But my air gave out along with my energy. I collapsed.

Lao Yang came up from behind, grabbed my hand, and pulled me with him. At last we reached the back of the waterfall. Suddenly the hundred-pound pressure on my head went away and I floated up to the water's surface, gasping for air.

We were surrounded by darkness. I could hear Lao Yang wheezing and coughing. He spat a few times and asked, "Are you okay? Looks like we've made it to the other side."

I couldn't stop coughing either. "Yes, but we're still in trouble. There's something wrong with the water in this pool. If we don't stop coughing, we'll probably die."

We groped about in the darkness as we swam forward. Then I heard the same noises that had startled me when I was trying to recover my flashlight, but this time the sound was very, very close.

"Watch out," I yelled to Lao Yang, "something's coming at us—oh shit!"

I felt a cold, slimy hand touch my shoulder. I dove underwater and kicked at the figure I found standing behind me. It released its grip, and I came back up to the surface and yelled, "Damn it, there's a ghost in this pool."

Lao Yang had found his waterproof lighter, ignited it, and turned to see what I was talking about. It would probably have been better if he hadn't. Behind us a pale head floated up from under the water, staring at us as if it wanted to eat us both alive.

We began paddling backward. Lao Yang tried to pull out his gun, but he was so frightened he couldn't.

The head rolled its eyes into its sockets so all we could see were the whites. It opened its mouth as though it wanted to speak and then it hurled itself toward me, pressing against my chest.

"Help, it's a fucking vampire!" I shrieked. Then I heard distinct words, "Help me—please help me."

I steeled myself, touched the head, and pushed it close to my own face. This was no ghost. Liang stared back at me, blubbering and pleading, his face ashen with exhaustion, his eyes rolling back into his head. I reached into the pool and grabbed him around his waist just as he began to sink below the water's surface.

"Help me," I called to Lao Yang.

"Damn it. How did this bastard get here?" Lao Yang yelled.

"He probably lost his group and didn't have the guts to go on his own, so he shadowed us. That's who I heard splashing around earlier."

"So what do we do with him now? This guy was with those killers. Is he going to give us trouble when he regains his strength?"

"We don't have a choice; we can't leave him to drown. Let's find a place where we can get back on dry land and deal with him later."

We swam on for another ten feet or so, pulling Liang behind us, when we came across a long, wide stone staircase under the water. It ascended all the way from the pool's bottom and ended about a dozen steps above the water. Slowly we climbed the steps and got out of the pool at last.

I was exhausted and collapsed at the top of the stairs, gasping for breath, but Lao Yang was manic with excitement. He took out the torches we had made with the gloves and driftwood, doused them with the bottle of wine that we'd taken from the dead student, and set them ablaze. I lifted my head to see where we were.

The entrance to the so-called world of the dead was nothing more than an average-size cave that looked as though it had been formed by nature and then disturbed by men.

Above the steps sat a platform made from layers of green rock that was surrounded by four stone pillars engraved with birds and animals. A tall bronze container stood placed in the middle of the platform. It looked like a large gourd bottle about a head taller than I was and was covered with spotted rust stains. The pattern of a double-bodied serpent and pictures of a sacrificial ceremony were carved on its outer surface.

This was an altar, I thought. The She clan placed more importance on sacrificial ceremonies than they did on the burial of their dead. Finding this bottle convinced me that we were getting close to the ancient tomb.

We walked onto the platform and put our backpacks and Liang's limp body down on the ground before inspecting the other side of the platform. There was a stone staircase the width of ten men, with at least one hundred steps that spiraled all the way down to the depths of the cave.

The flame from our makeshift torches wasn't strong enough to shine all the way to the bottom, and we couldn't make out what was underneath us. "If this is the entrance to the netherworld, then right here in front of us is its reception desk," I said to Lao Yang. "Below us is probably hell itself. Are you scared?"

Lao Yang pointed to the unconscious body of Liang and said, "Scared my ass. I can't wait to go down. But what are we going to do with this guy?"

"You know I'm as eager as you to take a look at the tomb's entrance but now that we're stuck with this jerk, we can't just abandon him. The least we can do is make sure he's regained his senses before we take off."

We slapped Liang's face and then gave him a few sips of wine. His face began to regain its color and Lao Yang pulled at his closed eyelids. "Can you talk now, asshole?"

Blinking rapidly, Liang nodded and coughed as he tried to reply.

"Don't be afraid. We're not the same as the gang you were hanging out with. We're not going to hurt you, unless you jeopardize our safety," Lao Yang told him. "Be straight with us and we'll take you with us. Fuck around and I'll smash your face in, understand?"

Liang nodded, opened his mouth to reply, and fell into

another coughing fit instead. Lao Yang poured a few more sips of wine into his mouth and removed his belt to tie tightly around Liang's wrists. "I'm still worried," he said. "These guys are all lawless. Let's tie him up before we do anything else."

Liang had no energy and let Lao Yang tie him up without putting up a fight. He didn't look as though he was going to present much of a problem. We got him to his feet, pushed him ahead of us, and the three of us made our way down the steep staircase, with Liang in front to absorb any traps that might be in our path.

At the bottom of the staircase was a black plank and directly beyond that lay a cliff, with total darkness below it.

"Well, fuck this," Lao Yang complained. "It would be fine if we still had our flashlights, but with only one small torch left to provide light, how the hell are we going to see what lies at the bottom of this cliff? What do we do now?"

Finally Liang spoke. "Gentlemen, I have a signal rifle that shoots flares in my bag."

Lao Yang quickly checked Liang's bag and announced, "He's not lying to us—maybe he's not so bad after all—at least he's cooperative."

I grabbed the rifle, released the safety, and then shot a signal flare to the top of the cliff. A trail of fire flashed by, lighting up a large area below. We looked down and were speechless.

A dozen feet below the cliff was a huge cave filled with piles of things that looked like dried firewood. But as we took a second look, we saw they were all bones, layers and layers of bones.

"What is this place?" I exclaimed. "Holy fuck, it's a

mass grave."

No wonder this place was believed to be the world of the dead. I was sure that I was staring straight into hell but I also knew I'd seen this before, in the carcass cave near the cavern of blood zombies.

There had to be some sort of connection between this place and the carcass cave, but how was that possible, separated as the two places were by hundreds of years and hundreds of miles? They both held the same piles of neatly stacked human bones and the hexagonal bells too. Would we soon find a crystal coffin and a corpse of a beautiful woman in white in this place as we had in that other cavern? I began to glance around nervously, looking for corpse-eating insects crawling around the bones.

Liang's signal flare was near the end of its arc and as it flickered and died, I glimpsed something in the middle of the stack of bones. "Set off another flare," I yelled. "I saw something weird down there."

CHAPTER SEVENTEEN

REST

Lao Yang reloaded the signal gun and fired another flare in the same direction as the first. Its blaze of light showed a huge open space in the middle of the cave. It was empty of bone piles and sank downward.

"It's a pit, I'm sure," I shouted, "and it's at least sixty square feet. It's gigantic!"

"It looks exactly like the one I found with my cousin, where we found the bronze branch," Lao Yang yelled. "We made it!"

The second flare died and once again we stood in darkness. "I'll set off another," Lao Yang said but I stopped him. "We've seen enough for now—no reason to waste our resources."

"What should we do now? Should we take a look around or wait for morning?"

"So far everything Old Man Liu told us is true. After all, we found the chain that led us here safely so I'm sure this tomb is filled with treasure. But we need to be cautious. Places with piles of corpses mean big trouble and we need to be prepared for things that you haven't even seen in your worst nightmares." I wanted to tell him what we had found in the carcass cave but I knew it would send Lao

Yang shrieking back up the waterfall so I shut up.

I recalled what we had seen under the light of the flare just moments before. To get to that pit, we would have to climb at least sixty feet down that cliff without any rock-climbing equipment, not even a rope.

Then we'd have to walk through the piles of bones and pray there were no zombies lurking about. That didn't seem too probable since I saw no bodies that held flesh, only skeletons and dismembered bones. But some of the skulls of the skeletons I had just seen bore cruel and terrifying grimaces. No human face could possibly convey that degree of viciousness; why, I wondered, were these skulls frozen in this much horror?

A sound drew our attention and we saw Liang crawling toward the stone staircase. Lao Yang raised his gun and bellowed, "One more step back and I'll shoot both of your kneecaps and throw you over the cliff."

Liang obviously thought this was an empty threat so he made a lunge for the stairs. Lao Yang sent a bullet ricocheting off one of the steps. The whine of the bullet turned to a horrible scream as it echoed through the cave and Liang curled up into a ball. "Don't kill me," he squealed, "I won't try to escape, I promise—just don't shoot at me again."

"Get over here before I lose my temper and blow your useless head off," Lao Yang raged.

Liang crawled back and squatted next to us. "Gentlemen, you can see I'm just a consultant, tagging along with Old Tai to make a living. Please let me go. You're on the verge of making a fortune and I don't have the strength to kill a chicken. I'm no help at all; I'll only slow you down."

"Did you really think we want to take you with us?" Lao Yang sputtered. "Go—get the fuck out of here, but drop that backpack. We need it. In fact I'll kill you for it if I have to."

"But this bag belongs to me. There's a saying that gentlemen—"

Lao Yang waved the gun in his hand. "I'm no gentleman. I'm an animal, straight out of prison. No point in blabbering your intellectual bullshit to me."

Liang seemed pretty damned shrewd, I thought. If we let him go and he ran into Uncle Tai and the others, they'd be after us in no time. We needed to keep this guy where we could see him.

"My turn to talk now," I told Lao Yang and turned to Liang. "Our situation right now isn't exactly the bed of roses and lilies you seem to think it is. And even if we let you leave with your precious backpack, you'd never get out of here alive on your own. You almost died in the pool before we found you, after all. Why don't we do this—you come down with us and take a look. If there's any treasure, we'll give you the same share you'd get from Old Tai. If the three of us stick together, we'll all have a better chance of surviving."

Lao Yang interrupted, "If you don't want to go down with us, that's all right too. Just leave everything behind—and take off all your clothes before you go."

"Don't, don't jump to any conclusions. We can discuss this. Since you two gentlemen think so highly of me, it would be inappropriate for me to decline any offer you might throw in my direction. And with my knowledge and your experience, we could make a good team."

I grabbed Liang's bag and turned it upside down, looking for something useful like some rope or a flashlight, but all he had was food and clothing.

"Uncle Tai carried everything important," Liang told us. "I was only given a flare gun so I could send up a signal if I got lost."

"Since we have no ropes, the only way we're going to get down this cliff is by turning into geckos with sticky feet," Lao Yang said. "Who knows if it's even possible to climb down this thing? It looks steeper than hell to me."

I fired a flare downward and it followed the wall of the cliff, showing crevices and ledges where we could put our feet as we climbed. "This would be easy, if we only had some light," I decided.

It was close to midnight and we knew we all needed to get some sleep and make our descent after we'd rested. If we tried to do it tonight, we might as well just leap over the edge, since we were sure to die anyway.

I began to wonder if Uncle Tai and the chubby guy from Guangdong were still alive, and if they were, if they still had their guns. Running into them would mean a fight and we had to keep our eyes open and our wits sharp as we traveled on. I wanted to ask Liang about his companions but decided he probably wasn't ready to tell me the truth yet. I was sure he didn't trust us any more than we did him. Who knew? He was probably waiting for his old pals to show up and rescue him.

Meanwhile Lao Yang was mulling over more practical matters. "I hate this place. I can feel those corpses staring at me. Let's go back up to the sacrificial platform and sleep there."

"Fine idea," I agreed and we climbed back up the stairs,

where Lao Yang made a fire and cooked some food. He and Liang fell asleep soon after eating but I kept watch, my gun close at hand. When Lao Yang woke to take the second shift, I slept badly and woke up five hours later feeling worse than ever.

While we ate breakfast, I noticed Liang's face wasn't as guarded as he had looked the day before. "Tell me about Old Tai and the others," I asked him.

Liang was no fool and he knew why I was curious. "Since we're on the same side now, I'll tell you the truth. Of the five of us, only Uncle Tai and his nephew knew what the hell they were doing. Boss Lee and Boss Wang were the moneybags financing it all and I just tagged along. I wanted to see the excavation process and the two bosses said I could have a share in any treasure we found."

"Just a minute," Lao Yang broke in. "You say there were five of you but we only saw four once you were on the road. Where's the fifth guy?"

"Oh, you mean Boss Lee. When we were in the tunnel he went off to wash his face in the stream. We found him later; something had bitten his head right off his neck."

"That's enough about that," I said, and Lao Yang and I both struggled to keep from puking up our breakfasts. We'd seen Boss Lee's head and the memory of it in the stomach of the Siberian salmon wasn't one we wanted to think about.

"Tell me about Boss Lee and Boss Wang," I said, wanting to change the subject quickly.

"I can tell you what I know, which isn't as much as you would probably like. Do you think you can trust my information?"

"Start talking," I said, and Liang began his story.

17. REST

CHAPTER EIGHTEEN

THE CLIMB

"The two guys from Guangdong were Wang Qi and Lee Pipa, both of them well established in the local antique trade. Wang wasn't as educated or as cultured as Mr. Lee but he had a photographic memory, which made him a valuable partner. I have no idea of how the two of them found each other but they made a formidable team."

"Why did they have to come on this journey with you? Why couldn't they just give you some information, send you off, and relax in peace and comfort at home?" I asked.

"Don't you understand? This is the problem with having too much money: wealthy men have no challenges in their daily lives and have to waste money to get a feeling of self-worth beyond what's in their bank accounts. They're buying excitement because they're half-dead with boredom," Lao Yang sneered.

Liang smiled. "I thought the same thing at first, but later I found out that their motivations weren't so simple. Both of them were very determined to come with us. I think they had a secret reason for facing the dangers of this journey, one that will only be understood when we reach the tomb they were seeking."

"You know so much. Did you read the book that Mr. Lee

had with him? Do you know where the tomb lies?" I asked.

"That book was Lee Pipa's greatest treasure; I wasn't even allowed to glimpse its contents, and when he died it was snatched up by Mr. Wang. But I have a strong feeling based on other texts I've read in the past that the entrance to that tomb will be found under the piles of bones."

We finished our breakfast, picked up our backpacks, and loosened the belt around Liang's hands. Together the three of us walked to the edge of the cliff and began our descent.

The funny thing was that I was the most experienced of the three of us, so I was the one in the lead, carrying the torch. I was just a novice grave robber—how was it that I was in charge? Uncle Three would laugh his ass off if he could see me right now, I told myself gloomily.

But I had no choice but to take the responsibility I'd been given, even if I secretly thought I was unsuited for it. Step by step, I slowly led the way down the cliff, heading for the darkness at its base.

There were a few times I almost fell, but overall, although the cliff was quite steep, it wasn't a difficult descent. With courage and caution, even a little girl could do this—and perhaps more rapidly and less cautiously than we did.

Our relief at touching the ground was tarnished by the grimacing skeletons that surrounded us. Their bones were blackened by mildew and their musty odor choked our lungs as we breathed. It looked as though some of the corpses had been mutilated, and many of them had long fangs growing from where their mouths had once been.

Liang stepped right on top of a skull and broke its rotting bones. He wiped away the sweat that was dripping down his nose and shuddered. "I'm too old for this game. Go ahead and laugh at me if you like."

"Don't worry. We're all going to do things we wished we hadn't before we reach the end of this journey," I told him and raised my torch high to see where we were.

Skeletons were piled high, with a path leading through the mountains of bones. We couldn't see very far with only one torch to light the darkness, but earlier from the top of the cliff we had seen a trail leading toward the open pit. "We just have to keep going straight ahead," I decided, and Lao Yang nodded.

Liang was exhausted and unable to move. While he rested, I took a look at the skeletons. I turned after a few minutes and saw that Liang looked more interested than I had ever seen him before.

"What's on your mind?" I asked him.

He replied, "Some of these skeletons don't look human. The bone structure of their skulls doesn't look right."

"What the fuck? Just what would they be if they weren't human? Don't tell me we have zombies to deal with here."

"I can't tell right now. If you guys really want to know, I'd need to look at a few more. It's better if you find one that hasn't completely rotted away—maybe in the middle of this pile of skeletons here. Do you want to go take a look?"

Lao Yang growled, "You make it sound so easy and simple. But if these skeletons aren't human, we are all three of us completely fucked if we mess around in that pile and draw the attention of zombies. I say we keep on going and leave those bones untouched."

"Lao Yang's right. We're not on a scientific expedition, after all," I said.

"Forget it," Liang agreed, "I was only babbling. Pay no attention to what I said."

Our torch was burning quickly and would go out soon. If we were stuck here in the dark, we were done for. It was time to move on—and fast.

"We need to get out of here unless you'd like to cuddle up to a skeleton tonight," I said, and we all began to walk swiftly down the path that was lined with the bones of dead men.

Somehow I was reassured by seeing stone statues mixed in the piles of bones; I had no idea why. We walked through sticky, smelly mud and it occurred to me that it could be rotting flesh, not wet dirt. I tried to put that thought from my mind and didn't share it with my companions.

Our torch grew dimmer, we began to run, and I became confused. When we had looked at the pit from the top of the cliff, it seemed no farther away than half a mile at the most, a distance we should have easily covered in five minutes. But we had been walking for more than a quarter of an hour and we still hadn't reached it. Was that because we were walking through semidarkness or had we taken a wrong turn somewhere along the way?

We ran forward for another five minutes but nothing changed; we were still surrounded by piles of bones and only darkness stretched beyond them. "Where are we going and what have I done?" I muttered, hoping the others didn't hear.

Liang was wheezing for breath and pulled me to a stop. "Stop…running. There's no…point—we've been tricked, I'm quite sure."

CHAPTER NINETEEN

AN ARRAY OF CORPSES

"What the hell are you talking about?" Lao Yang asked, but less fiercely than he usually spoke to Liang.

While rubbing the left side of his chest, Liang pointed to the ground and asked, "Take a look at this bone here. Doesn't this look familiar?"

I lifted our flickering torch. There was a skull on the ground with a hole in its top, just like the one Liang had stepped on when he came down the cliff.

Lao Yang looked around and complained, "Where did you lead us, mighty torchbearer? Isn't this just where we started from?"

"Fuck you," I snapped, "I have no idea. This all looks the same no matter how far you travel along this path. I wasn't taking notes when we walked. Maybe we took a wrong fork in the road that led us back here."

Liang's breathing had gone back to normal and he looked more confident. He waved his hand at us and said, "No, that's not the problem. You guys weren't paying attention as you walked but I did. The path has been straight every step of the way; there was no turn or fork on the road. It's not that simple—we've been tricked."

Lao Yang's face turned the same color as the whites

of his eyes. "Shit, maybe the spirits of the bodies that died here are trying to keep us from reaching their holy ground?"

Liang shook his head. "I don't think so. I'm carrying something that has been blessed in a sacred ceremony. You guys might be kept from the holy area but I wouldn't."

"Liang, your insight in this case is much deeper than ours," I said. "What do you think is going on? Our torch won't last much longer and when the fire goes out, we'll be lost here forever. We have to find a way out as quickly as possible."

"In my opinion," Liang responded, "the reason why we're walking around in circles is because of the way the bone piles have been arranged. Thousands of bones have been placed in a crisscross pattern, which has turned the cave into a maze. You've both read the novels that tell how armies in past history trapped hundreds and thousands of troops inside a circle just by using a few stones. It's a piece of cake to trap the three of us with the piles of bones in here."

Both Lao Yang and I knew these stories, but that was an exaggeration to make novels impossible to put down. In real life how could rocks be so powerful and effective—if the stories were true why did we need things like tanks and artillery?

Lao Yang was obviously thinking the same thing. "Don't you mess around with us in the same way Boss Lee and Boss Wang tried to fool you. Sure, I've read those stories but they were stories, nothing more. Besides, when we looked down from the cliff, we saw no special patterns in the bone piles. How did things change once we were here? It's not as though the bones were commanded to go into formation."

Liang said, "What you saw from above is less complex than what actually is here. You had a quick peek at the path before we came down the cliff and once we got here much of what surrounded us was shrouded in darkness. Don't underestimate the craftiness of those who lived before us."

The man made sense, I had to admit. There was definitely something bizarre going on here.

"How can we reach the burial pit? Do you have a plan?" I asked.

Liang sighed. "I'm not trying to boast but this sort of problem is a cinch for me. With time I can figure out how to circumvent what's been done here, but I'm not sure we have time, since our torch is ready to go out. And we have something more important to decide right now."

I knew what he meant and it gave me a headache. Our main problem wasn't the confusion posed by the array of corpses but what we ought to do. We couldn't go back but it might be even worse to go forward. There were no villages or grocery shops in either direction and once our torch went out, we were sure to starve to death.

We watched the torch grow dim without saying a word. Then Lao Yang yelled, "Hey, I know! Let's set these bones ablaze. That will clear away the confusion and give us some light as well."

"Where do you come up with this bullshit? These bones are so rotten they'll never catch fire. And if they did, the smoke from them would suffocate us all. Forget it. I'll start walking and you guys watch the motion of the torch. If I stop going straight ahead, tell me and then we'll know where the problem is."

"No way," Lao Yang argued. "What if the torch goes out when you're halfway there? You can't go alone. Who's going to rescue you? We need to stay together in this place."

Before I could object to what he said, the torch flickered twice and then went out. We were in total darkness, surrounded by human bones.

CHAPTER TWENTY

IN THE DARK

The minute we were engulfed in darkness, Liang screamed. We heard his footsteps race away; a loud thump followed by a whimper told us he'd probably bumped into something that stopped his flight.

I groped for a lighter and relit the torch. There was still a lot of wood left to feed the flame—why had it gone out? There was no breeze in the cave so it hadn't been extinguished by any sort of air current.

I raised the torch to check on Liang, who had crashed into one of the skeletons, sending its bones flying all over the place. He sprawled near his scene of destruction, looking shaken and pale. Lao Yang and I helped him to his feet. "You're quite the grave robber," Lao Yang taunted. "Wish I had the nerves that you do—nothing rattles you, does it?"

"I'm not afraid of the dark but just as the torch went out, I felt air coming from somewhere, a gust of it right on my neck. It was cold and damp, like the breath of a zombie, and I ran."

Lao Yang laughed. "Cold air my ass, it was probably your own cold sweat dripping down your neck. If a zombie were behind you, it would go for your throat, not breathe on your neck."

"He's right," I agreed. "Try to relax a little. You can't panic like that every time you imagine a zombie is at your back."

Liang looked even more worried as we tried to reassure him. "Gentlemen, please believe me for all our sakes. There was something near me when the torch went out. It's not only the three of us in here."

He looked sincere as he tried to convince us and I knew he might be right. There was no reason for the torch to die, I had already figured that out that for myself.

"Come on, let's go take a look around," I said to Lao Yang and, holding out our guns, we walked toward the spot where Liang had stood when we were suddenly swept into darkness. Close to where he had been was a statue. We peered behind it but there was nothing there, and no footprints indicated that anyone had been there.

Lao Yang rolled his eyes and we turned away. A loud poof echoed near the statue and the torch in my hand went out once more.

"Shit," Lao Yang yelled, "watch out—there's something here. Light your torch again!"

I groped for my lighter but before I could find it, I was struck from behind by a wind so powerful that it brought me to my knees. It swept past my scalp and knocked me flat on the ground.

I wasn't hurt but in my fall I knocked down several statues and made one hell of a noise, which made Liang scream once more. I'm going to have to kill that coward, if Lao Yang doesn't beat me to it, I thought, and then realized I felt quite a bit like screaming myself.

I had to force myself to relight the torch but I did it as fast as I could. Liang and Lao Yang were both lying on the ground, looking as though they were ready to piss themselves. Except for that, and the damaged statues, everything looked the same as it had a minute ago. There were no footprints, no sign that anybody had been near us.

"Damn it," I said. "Could you be right, Liang? Have we antagonized a ghost?"

There was no reply. Liang looked as though he was in a coma. I tried to help him up but his bones were like soup and wouldn't support him. Lao Yang muttered, "Fuck this," and slapped Liang's face hard. It worked.

"What have I done? Why didn't I stay home? Why did I follow grave robbers? I'm going to die in a strange place, I'm done for, this is the end of me—oh no—" and then Lao Yang slapped him again.

"Stop this at once. Show the wisdom you should have acquired by now and stop blubbering like a child. Keep this up and we'll leave you here in the dark, you shameless coward." Then he asked me, "Did you see anything? What the hell was that? Do you think it was a zombie?"

"Zombies can't move that fast," I told him but he was ready to argue as usual.

"With all of these skeletons, there must be a corpse somewhere and where there's a corpse, there could be a zombie. I've heard there are different classes of zombies—maybe we've found one who has kung fu flying skills."

"Oh shit, you're a bigger jerk than the esteemed Mr. Liang who loves to whimper in corners. I don't have time to listen to your idiocy."

I walked over to the skeleton that Liang had knocked to

bits and poked at the bones with the barrel of my pistol. "Look at this. The air in this cave is so damp and humid that these bones are black with mildew. There's no way in hell that a zombie could exist in a place where flesh turns into the mud beneath our feet. If it turns out that I'm wrong you can tear off my head and feed it to your kung fu zombie, okay?"

Liang had regained his sanity. He blew his nose and announced, "It really doesn't matter whether this is the right environment for a zombie or not. We should take advantage of the light from our torch while we still have it and climb back up that cliff. Then we can think over what to do next."

I patted him on the shoulder. "Glad you're thinking clearly again but we're going to move on, not retreat. We have a goal and we're going to reach it."

"Don't worry, old man. We still have our guns; we'll protect you," Lao Yang said with a dash of sarcasm.

"Stop patronizing me," Liang snuffled. "If we run into zombies, a couple of guns aren't going to help."

"Oh hell, a zombie is made of flesh and flesh won't withstand a bullet. We're going on. There's nothing here that's frightening, only a wind that blows out our torch every five seconds but that's annoying, not life-threatening. Get ready to move," I ordered.

Lao Yang pulled Liang into a walking position and once again the three of us trudged down the path lined by the array of skeletons. Our footprints were still visible in the mud and we followed our previous route, which went straight ahead with no turns or forks in the road.

We walked for hours and then our landscape changed.

There were still skeletons but some of them had deteriorated to the point that they had lost their arms or legs; some of them even had rotting flesh still clinging to their bones.

Then with a loud bang one of them broke into pieces as though it had exploded, its skull rolling toward us. And with a poof our torch went out for the third time.

I braced myself in a squatting position for the gust of air that had knocked me off my feet before. But instead I heard Lao Yang's triumphant voice yell, "Holy shit! I've caught it! Light that fucking torch now," and something kicked me right in the face.

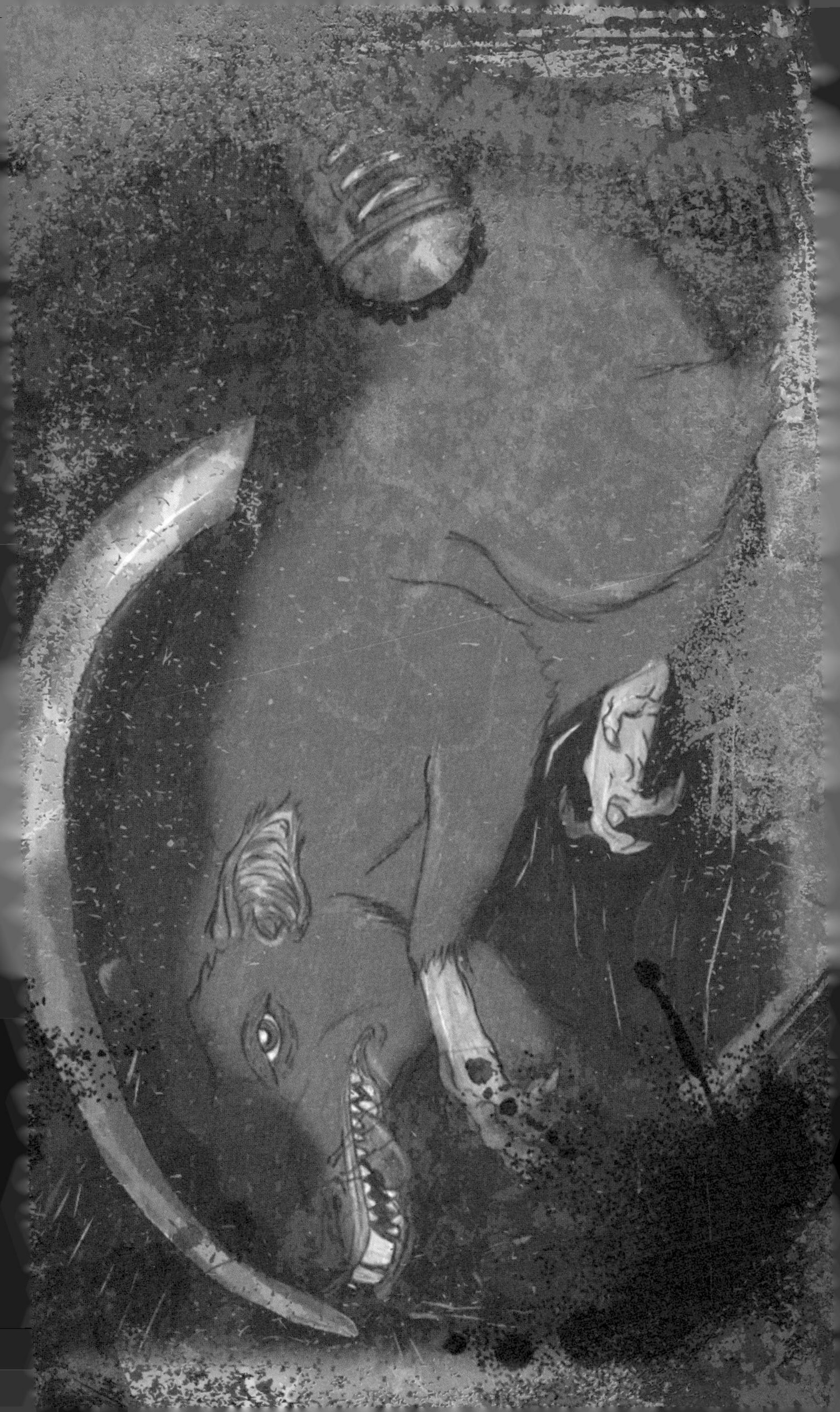

CHAPTER TWENTY-ONE

THE BONES

I could hear the crash of bones hitting the ground as I reeled backward. Regaining my balance, I set the torch ablaze one more time. There was Lao Yang fighting with something I couldn't see among a pile of skeletons, and bones and skulls were scattered everywhere.

I rushed over to join the fight but I was useless. Whatever Lao Yang was struggling with wasn't huge but it was horribly strong. Lao Yang weighed over two hundred pounds but his bulk did nothing to stop the creature he battled with. They twisted and crashed as they fought and there was no way I could get close to them.

But Lao Yang's strength was flagging and his opponent almost got away a couple of times. "Damn you, Liang—get over here and help," I yelled, and the two of us threw ourselves on top of Lao Yang, adding our weight to his.

"Get up, you're crushing every bone in my spinal cord," he mumbled.

Whatever was beneath the three of us had almost stopped struggling. "Do you think it's dead yet?" I gasped.

"I don't know," Lao Yang hissed, purple-faced, "but I almost am. Get the fuck off me."

I eased my pressure and Lao Yang sighed. "Did you have

to be so damn rough? We're not in our teens anymore, you know. I thought I was going to turn into a paraplegic, thanks to your brilliant solution."

"Oh shut up. If you knew how to fight, I wouldn't have had to rescue you. Now let's see what had you beaten to a pulp and whining like a little girl."

Lao Yang got to his feet. Beneath him was a hairy grey body, the size of a large dog, squashed like a bug and still quivering in its death throes. Lao Yang picked up a leg from one of the broken skeletons and turned the body over. "Fuck me," he said, "it's a giant rat."

The three of us looked at each other and started to laugh hysterically. "No wonder it always got away from us and we saw no footprints. It probably crawled into a hole in the cave wall the second after it attacked. So this was our ghost," Lao Yang hooted.

But then the same thought struck both him and me at the same time and from the look on Liang's face, he had already figured this out—how did a rat get to be this size anyway? It had to have been feeding on human flesh—and if there was one, there would probably be more. A pack of these would be deadly.

"We're dead. We've probably killed the rat king and his tribe is going to be out for our blood. Just think of those damned monkeys and what they almost did to us," Lao Yang said. "Let's get out of here now."

He turned to lead the way and then stopped. "Oh hell, which way should we go?"

In our battle when we had rolled head over heels, we lost our bearings and it was impossible to tell which way we had come from and where we wanted to go. Our path had turned dry long ago and we could no longer follow our trail of footprints in the stinking mud.

I turned to ask Liang's advice but he was wandering about picking up bones and humming a little tune. "Get over here," I hissed to Lao Yang. "This guy's losing it."

Our war with the giant rat had destroyed more than a dozen skeletons. Only a few bones were still in one piece, and those Liang was picking up and piling carefully together in a corner.

"What the fuck are you up to now?" Lao Yang bellowed.

"It's great!" Liang yelled back. "I've figured it out. Take a look, you two, and tell me what you see." He held a bone close to our faces and grinned like an idiot.

"You can stop your little game right now," Lao Yang told him. "We're not rag and bone men. If you're such an expert, then enlighten us so we can get going again."

Liang looked a little embarrassed. "Sorry. I'm too excited to choose my words carefully. Just take a look at this spot on the bone, please."

He placed the bone in my hand and I examined the spot he pointed at. "I don't see anything extraordinary here," I said. "The bone obviously was broken in this place but why is that so interesting?"

"This is a collarbone and the man it belonged to died from a broken neck. What you see here is what killed him—quickly and cleanly, the way you'd snap the neck of a rabbit."

"So what? So he died of a broken neck—poor thing," Lao Yang sneered. "Now can we get out of here before our torch burns out?"

"Just give me three more minutes—I promise you it will

be worth your while. Just listen, please."

"All right, talk, damn it. Lao Yang, shut the hell up," I ordered.

"Right—look at this. The man who died had his throat cut and so did all seven of the collarbones that I've just found here. And their throats weren't cut from behind as was usual during burials where human sacrifices took place. These men died in battles, not as sacrificial offerings."

Liang's eyes looked like a maniac's as he explained his theory and I felt a bit frightened. Why was he getting so worked up over this? So the skeletons had been killed in battle? So what? Were we going to have to kill this jerk and add his bones to the pile just so we could shut him up?

"So, yes, right, of course…is this the big discovery you've just made?" I asked in soothing tones, glaring at Lao Yang to keep him from exploding.

"Not at all," Liang replied. "The discovery is this." He plucked something from his pile of bones and handed it to me. "It's hidden inside this thing."

What he gave me looked like a rain hat with a wide brim, but it was too heavy to be a hat. I raised the torch and looked carefully. "Is this bronze? Is it part of a suit of armor?"

"That's right," Liang nodded, looking very pleased with himself. "It was made around the time of the Han dynasty."

"Can you tell me," I asked, "if this armor was worn by Han people who died when wearing it, why were they in a burial pit that had been dug thousands of years before they were ever alive? The She clan had died out millennia before the Han came into power. What does this mean?"

"If I'm correct, this place wasn't a sacrificial pit, it was a battlefield. The corpses here are divided into two factions. One group guarded the tomb. The others were soldiers in the Han army. Remember the legend of the deaf-mute army that disappeared in the Gate to Hell? The men the emperor used to rob graves, since they could never tell anyone about what they found? I believe the She clan didn't die out, they intermarried with outsiders and lost their history and culture—except for a group that guarded this tomb. Somehow I think the deaf-mute army found out about them, broke their way into this cavern, and stormed into this burial pit. They killed everyone who guarded the place, and many of them died as well. We're surrounded by their ghosts."

Liang fell silent and I glanced nervously at our guttering torch. Don't go out, I thought as I watched it diminish to the size of a candle flame, this is no time to stand in the dark.

CHAPTER TWENTY-TWO

FIRE DRAGON

"We may have been the first men to come here since the day these corpses fell in battle." Liang observed. "I think we can't find our way through them because the spirits in this place have made it their job to confuse us. Do you two have any idea of how to get past them?"

"My cousin told me that if we ever came across a place like this, we could find our way out if we tied red string to our left feet. But we have nothing red, do we?" Lao Yang asked. "Maybe we should cut ourselves and smear our blood on our feet?"

"Are you crazy? The last thing we need is for these spirits to get a whiff of our blood. Think of something else," I told him.

"We need some light," Liang said. "Let's send up one of our signal flares and then move fast."

"Not a bad idea," I replied. "Send up a flare, Lao Yang." He fired and we all looked up, waiting for it to blaze into light. Instead it made an explosive sound and fell straight down to the floor of the cave without catching fire.

"Shit," Lao Yang muttered. "It stopped at the roof of the cave before it ignited."

But it did burst into flame, there on the cavern floor—

the heat was almost overwhelming and we knew it would burn for almost a minute at a hellish temperature.

"We're in trouble," Liang shouted. "Look at that."

The flame shot upward in a wall of fire and raced down the cleared path space between the piles of bones. In the middle of it was a flaming dragon that slithered through the blaze unscathed by the inferno.

Lao Yang bent down, scooped some of the dirt from the cavern's floor, and sniffed at it. "Holy shit," he shrieked, "this dirt is soaked with kerosene!"

I picked up some dirt and held it to my nose. He was right. How had we managed to trigger this particular trap, anyway?

The fire dragon kept racing through the fire which now formed two walls, each taller than we were. The cave was full of light now and I clearly saw a network of open paths leading through the array of skeletons, all joining together in an interlinking patchwork. Soon the fire dragon would make his way to where we stood—there had to be some way out. I peered around with the instinct of a trapped rat and saw a spot not yet alive with flame only a short distance away, separated from us by a wall of fire.

The fire dragon was coming close and moving fast. "Follow me!" I yelled, and the three of us began racing through the piles of bones and vaulting past the stone statues. As we approached the fire wall, we could smell our own hair burning and hot air scorched our faces—but we couldn't stop. Adrenaline forced us through the flames. I closed my eyes and screamed as I hit the ground and rolled to extinguish the fire that burned my clothes.

When I opened my eyes, there were Liang and Lao

Yang, rolling beside me. One of Lao Yang's eyebrows was gone, but he looked as though he'd live to continue his habit of pissing me off. Liang was in trouble; he couldn't seem to extinguish his own flames no matter how much he rolled about on the ground. I rushed over to help him, covering his body with dirt until the fire went out.

He kept screaming in pain but Lao Yang and I tore open his shirt and saw that his burns weren't serious. Then I began to look around at our situation.

The fire wall barricaded our sanctuary from the outer cave area, which was a blazing hell. The heat of the fire was cracking the skeletons and sending bone fragments into the air like shrapnel. The cave was sure to soon be completely destroyed by the flames and the oxygen in here would quickly be exhausted. We were bound to suffocate or burn to death—or both.

"Oh hell! Look over there," Lao Yang shrieked and I turned to see seven giant rats leaping toward us through the fire wall—all of them badly burned and completely pissed off. I ducked and Lao Yang began to shoot—one of them fell motionless. I raised our burned-out torch to use as a club, battering several, but another dozen rushed forward to replace them.

One landed on my back, claws raking my flesh, and I fell. Lao Yang fired again. I looked up as the rat on my back plummeted to the ground and then yelled—outside the wall of fire was a crowd of rats, all of them plainly aware that safety lay in our direction. Once they all leaped past the flames, we would be dead meat.

"Stop shooting!" I yelled at Lao Yang. "It's a waste of ammunition. We're going to have to think our way out of this."

"Look!" Liang shouted. "There's a tunnel over here!" And he was right—in the middle of where we stood there was an almost invisible opening in the center of the pit. Lao Yang handed me his rifle, grabbed Liang by the arm, and walked to the tunnel's entrance. I followed rapidly behind them.

We'd gone only a few steps when the rats closest to us screamed and rushed at us. Their eyes and fangs glowed in the darkness and Lao Yang yelled, "Shoot, damn it. Blow them straight to hell."

CHAPTER TWENTY-THREE

THE BRONZE TREE

I fired rapidly and the first group of rodents was blown to bits, stopping the ones behind them and giving us a chance to escape. We made it to the tunnel opening and looked down into another cave. Lao Yang squeezed Liang through the narrow opening and leaped in after him. "Come on," he called to me, and I jumped.

It was a short drop. I flicked on my lighter and saw Lao Yang standing nearby with Liang sprawled on the ground at our feet. There were torches set into crevices of the cavern walls. We lit them and had a look around.

We were in a small chamber with mural-covered walls and a ceiling inlaid with a mosaic of blue rocks. It was damp and smelled of mildew. There were a few primitive tools and weapons on the floor but no burial objects and no coffin, although marks on the floor made it plain that one had rested there at one time. No corridors led out of this room and I wondered why the skeletons above had died to protect this tiny, undistinguished spot?

We could feel the heat from the furnace above us and knew the oxygen available in our little refuge was going fast. This wasn't a place where we could linger, I knew, and I went to check on Liang.

He was unconscious, his body clammy and his breath shallow. I poured water into his mouth, hoping it would revive him. At the top of the opening, the rats gathered, shrieking and squealing and trying to force their way in. Lao Yang and I took everything lying about on the floor and crammed the objects into the cave entrance, grateful that many of the weapons had sharp blades and made a threatening barrier.

"I don't see any exits here," Lao Yang told me. "Do you suppose there might be a hidden passageway somewhere? If not, we're going to be a cooked meal for the rats in a few minutes."

Before I could reply, I heard something fall from the cave's entrance. A rat had managed to chew through one of the bricks, which fell at our feet. Fortunately the rat was stuck in the hole it had made and gibbered furiously as it stared down at us.

All the rats were now chomping away at the bricks, determined to get at us. I grabbed one of the ancient weapons, a bronze spear, and forced the rat's head back up through the hole it had made. Lao Yang took off his coat and used a spear to stuff it into the crack where the rat had been, but it was soon useless. A rat bit through it and a dozen of them swarmed down the spear into our chamber.

But instead of attacking they all rushed into one of the corners. "Damn it, they're looking for an escape route too! Let's follow them," Lao Yang yelled.

We ran to the corner as the rats disappeared through a hole at the base of the wall. Lao Yang grabbed a large copper chain that lay on the floor and smashed it near the opening; it cracked and broke to form a bigger opening that was the size of our heads. Through it we could see another stone chamber.

Lao Yang battered the wall with his chain, enlarging the opening. We grabbed Liang by the arms and climbed inside.

It was an empty room with a well in the middle that was deep and dry; the rats all jumped down into it without stopping for a second. We could hear the sound of bricks cracking in the chamber we had just left and we knew it was only minutes before this room collapsed from the heat of the fire above.

Lao Yang and I knew we had no choice but to pick up Liang and follow the rats. Once again we jumped, with me in the lead.

I slid, rolled, and landed on a flat surface. Knowing that Lao Yang and Liang were right behind me, I rolled some distance away from my landing space. They both came crashing down, right where I had been only seconds before. And then we heard a terrible roar and felt a wild trembling above us. The cave had collapsed.

Holding his head in his hands, Lao Yang sat up and asked me, "What is this place?"

I held up my lighter and saw we were still in the well, on a horizontal part of it. "We're in a water shaft. It looks as though it's part of a tomb's drainage system."

"And where do we go from here?" Lao Yang persisted.

"How the hell would I know? Did I bring a crystal ball with me when I agreed to come on this shit-quest with you?" I began to yell, just as several rats slid down the well, leaping from where they had landed on Lao Yang's shoulders and running down the passage ahead.

"Follow them—they know," I shouted as I raced after the rodents. They were fast and I almost lost them. Then I felt a breeze sweeping in front of me and in a flash the rats had vanished. The ground disappeared under my feet and I rolled down and then out of the water shaft, Lao Yang, with Liang on his back, close behind me. I raised my lighter.

We weren't in a tomb chamber. This was the gigantic circular bottom of a vertical tunnel, about two hundred feet or more in diameter. The bottom was shaped like a pit with torches placed around it. I quickly lit a few of them and the space flared into light.

This had clearly been made by men but why had they dug so deep? I could dimly make out a large object in the middle of it but I couldn't see it clearly. It was terribly hot in this place with boiling air blowing down from above and I felt dizzy and a bit stupid.

I held a torch high so Lao Yang could carry Liang into the pit. It was full of the same statues we had seen earlier, almost a hundred of them. In the middle of the pit was a massive bronze column, about thirty feet in diameter, looking almost like a curving wall of bronze. The column was firmly planted in the rocks at the bottom of the pit, looking almost as if it grew from that spot.

Hanging from the column were many tiny brass rods all of different thicknesses, at least a thousand near us and more above. The column looked exactly like a tree, I realized, one with many branches and a trunk emerging from the depths of the earth.

Liang had regained consciousness and said, "Whoever dug this tunnel obviously wanted to uproot this tree.

Look—they dug all the way to the bottom of the pit and still hadn't reached the end of this thing. Who knows how much more of this column is still below ground?"

I couldn't answer him. How could this be here? The She Kingdom didn't have the technology to cast a bronze piece this size. But who else could have made it? Had it sprouted up from hell?

Liang tapped my shoulder. I turned and saw Lao Yang, staring at the bronze tree with a hypnotized expression, moving toward it as though he were sleepwalking.

CHAPTER TWENTY-FOUR

CLIMBING

"Lao Yang, stop!" I yelled. We saw him shudder as he heard my voice and then come to a stop.

"Where were you going?" I asked as I ran to his side.

"I have no idea. I saw the tree and all I wanted to do was climb to its top."

"There's a weird feeling about this tree—an evil quality to it," Liang said. "Try not to touch it and don't stare at it."

"I hate to say it, but for once you're right," Lao Yang admitted, and I nodded. "I'm going to examine it. This is too rare to ignore. Watch closely and stop me if I begin to act peculiar, okay?"

I raised my torch and peered at the surface of the trunk. Engraved all over it were images of the double-bodied serpent. Liang stood beside me and said, "Look at all the snakes. Obviously this was used in sacred rituals, but who will ever know why?"

I began to think of what Mr. Lee had said about the treasures in this tomb surpassing those in the mausoleum of the First Emperor. But the only precious object we had found so far was this tree. Where were the other marvels that were supposed to be in this place?

"The tree," I yelled, and Liang and Lao Yang both looked

startled, moving toward me in case I did something stupid.

"I'm okay," I reassured them, "it's just that if there are treasures in this tomb, they're probably somewhere on this tree. And I bet you anything that the coffin is hidden on this bronze monster too. We need to climb it and have a look."

"You're right," Lao Yang agreed. "After all we're already here—climbing up a bit is no big deal. There are so many branches it's going to be as easy as climbing a staircase."

Liang was silent and I was sure he was going to back out of this part of our quest but when I looked at him, he was grinning and nodding. "Absolutely, this is our final challenge—we have to do this no matter what. Let's go."

We followed Lao Yang as he stepped onto a branch and pulled himself up to the next. "It looks easy but don't get careless," he warned as we made our ascent.

After what seemed like only a few minutes, I looked down at where we had begun our climb and could no longer see the pit. Liang was wheezing and coughing, making me realize we'd gone much farther than I'd thought. "Hang on," I called to Lao Yang, "let's take a little break before we go on."

Liang sank to his haunches, gasping for breath. Lao Yang looked at him and shook his head. "He's done for the day and we still have probably another three hundred feet to go before we get to the top of this thing. We're going to have to spend the night on the tree—might as well try to relax."

He rummaged around in his pack and found a box of biscuits. Passing them around as though he were at a tea party, he asked, "Tell me. Can we name this discovery after ourselves and can my name be first, since it was my idea to come here?"

24. CLIMBING

"Oh fuck you. We have one or two more important matters to consider here, like getting to the top of this thing before nightfall. I really don't agree that this is the right spot to spend the night, you know. Once we get to the top you can call this tree Shithead if you want to name it after yourself—I could give a damn."

"Don't make me laugh—it makes the tree shake," Lao Yang said. "Oh hell, what's going on now?' The entire tree moved back and forth, as if a strong wind had struck it, and Lao Yang cupped his hands together over one ear. Pressing it against the bronze trunk, he whispered, "Damn it, something's climbing up after us."

I suddenly thought of Uncle Tai but realized it was impossible for him to have made it through the collapsed cavern of bones. What was coming for us and how could we protect ourselves against it?

"Should we go down and make the first move?" Lao Yang whispered, and I shook my head. I took off my belt, tied our torch to a bronze branch, and motioned for Lao Yang and Liang to follow me into the shadows where the light didn't penetrate. If our pursuer looked up, all it would see would be the light from the torch and we would have the element of surprise on our side.

We stopped breathing and listened. We could feel a vibration that was irregular and very rapid, and a sound like scratching against the bronze surface. I tried not to think of the giant rats. Lao Yang raised his gun.

Dimly below us we could see shapes that looked human. Then Lao Yang gasped, "Climb up, damn it—hurry." Liang looked down and screamed. They both scrambled upward as though something was pushing them from behind.

I still couldn't see anything and peered below. Something was crawling up but I couldn't make out what it was. "Move, you bastard," Lao Yang roared down at me and I grabbed the torch and climbed in the direction of his voice.

We climbed like crazy things, faster and faster—until I bumped into something and came to a stop. It was Liang, clinging to a branch with sweat pouring down his face like a tiny waterfall. I moved past him in a panic, but he grabbed my leg as I pushed past.

"Don't leave me here," he begged, "help me climb up, please."

The minute I stopped, I lost my momentum, my adrenaline drained away, and my legs trembled so hard I could barely keep my balance. "Damn it, I can't climb anymore. I'm done. Forget it. Who cares what's coming after us? We have to fight it because we can't run from it. Where the fuck is Lao Yang?"

Liang pointed farther down the tree. When I looked in that direction, there was a man, climbing steadily toward us and it sure as hell wasn't Lao Yang.

CHAPTER TWENTY-FIVE

CRACKING

The closer the figure got to us the less certain I was that it was human. Its face was almost twice the size of any man's I'd ever seen and its features could have come from one of the stone figures below us, impassive, inexpressive, inhuman, lips upturned into a snarl. When it saw the torch that Liang brandished, it flinched and drew back.

Where is Lao Yang? I shivered. Could this creature have killed him? But he'd been carrying a rifle and would have fired it to defend himself against any attack. There'd been no gunshots; perhaps he was hiding.

The face had almost reached my feet. Liang screamed and scurried up the tree when he saw what was climbing toward us. Without thinking, I pulled the trigger of my pistol; the head exploded and its body fell back into the darkness. But before I could feel relieved, two more faces rose up from the blackness like twin moons. As I struggled to reload my pistol, a hand tapped me on the shoulder.

One of the faces had moved behind me and because Liang had taken the torch with him, I could barely see it. I had no other way to defend myself; I head-butted its face with all my strength.

The head was as hard as a boulder and I almost lost my grip when I struck it. "Get out of the way," a voice yelled and Lao Yang appeared from the shadows beneath me. He fired. A stream of flame passed me with a roar, striking the bronze trunk with a shower of sparks, just inches from my head.

Lao Yang fired a volley of bullets. None of them hit their targets and fortunately none hit me. I dodged right and left, hoping I'd survive my rescue. But it did buy me some time and I used it to reload my own firearm, thinking I might have to use it to stop Lao Yang's crazed marksmanship. Instead one of the giant faces came into view and I shot it, sending it into midair and crashing to the ground.

I looked for Lao Yang but instead saw at least ten more giant faces coming at me all at the same time, climbing with the speed and agility of monkeys. What are these damned things? I wondered, just as one grabbed me by the leg and began pulling me down while another crawled up to my side.

With no time to reload my pistol, I used it to bludgeon the face of the monster that was beside me but it didn't seem to feel a thing. It was poised to attack but a loud snapping sound echoed close by and a large crack appeared on its face. It reeled backward and I rapidly jammed more bullets into the chamber of my pistol.

Quickly I fired at the creature that pulled on my ankle and its head shattered, but its hand still clutched my leg in a death grip. Its weight was more than I could withstand and I knew I was about to plunge to my death.

Before I could lose my own grip, help came from an

unexpected source—the monster with the cracked face grabbed me by the throat and pulled me up toward him. Suffocating from his grip, I once again hammered my pistol in the direction of its head.

The creature moved in a frenzied attempt to avoid my blows but I managed to strike it on the spot where the crack had appeared. It screamed, leaped to a higher branch, and began to scrabble frantically at its face.

Without its support, my hands loosened and I dropped three feet before I grabbed a branch to stop my fall. I looked up and saw the monster's face had broken into tiny white fragments that fell about me like snowflakes. Catching one as it drifted past, I found it was a bit of stone. Shit, are these moving statues? I wondered. But when I looked at the monster above me, I saw it now wore another face covered with yellow fur.

"Lao Yang," I bellowed, "I know what the hell these things are. They're those monkeys!"

From the darkness below I heard Lao Yang shout, "Monkeys my ass! How could there monkeys with human faces?"

"Those aren't human faces—they're masks made from stone."

"Fuck this—what difference does it make what they are? Can we kill them all?"

We both opened fire and picked off at least five of the figures climbing up to get us. The others fell back as the dead monkeys plummeted past them, and Lao Yang and I climbed away from them as fast as we could.

"Shit, they really are monkeys," Lao Yang gasped. "What the hell is going on here?"

25. CRACKING

About ten feet up the tree we found Liang, unconscious from terror, lying on a thick cluster of branches that kept him from falling to the ground, with his torch still aflame and jammed securely between three branches. Lao Yang picked up the torch and raised it high. A crowd of monkeys was swarming up the tree and he muttered, "We're fucked, I'm out of bullets and you must be close to the same situation yourself. At least we know they're afraid of fire."

He waved the torch menacingly and the monkeys stopped their ascent. But when they saw it wasn't coming near them, they pressed forward again. "Move," Lao Yang shouted and I grabbed for Liang's arm. It was limp and almost lifeless.

"Forget him; he's been nothing but a pain in the ass since we first took him on. Let's go," Lao Yang urged me. As much as I wanted to agree with him, I couldn't leave Liang but I couldn't move him either.

I had four bullets left, and the ones in the chamber killed several monkeys. I loaded the last two but before I could shoot, Liang grabbed my arm and whispered, "Don't waste your bullets. Use the signal flares."

Lao Yang heard him and immediately pulled out the signal gun. I grabbed it and shot at the rock wall some distance from the bronze tree. The flare bounced off the wall, ricocheted back to the tree, and exploded in the middle of the cluster of monkeys. Quickly I set off two more flares and we were surrounded by dazzling white light.

"Close your eyes," I shouted. "This is too close—it could blind us."

The heat scorched through our eyelids and the smell of burning flesh filled the air. We could hear the monkeys shrieking in agony and when we finally opened our eyes, they had disappeared.

My eyeballs felt as though they had been blistered, Lao Yang had rivulets of tears rolling down his cheeks, and Liang was unconscious again. If I weren't still holding him by his shirt collar, he would be in pieces at the bottom of the tree. But at least the monkeys were gone. The ones that hadn't been incinerated in the heat were certain to be blind by now. This made the pain in my own eyes seem quite bearable and I cheered up.

I propped Liang into an upright position and then went to check on Lao Yang, who was squinting, spitting, and swearing. His eyes finally focused on me and he cursed, "You son of a bitch, you never give a man any warning before you launch one of your brilliant plans. I'll kill you if it turns out that I'm blind because of you."

"Of all the fucking nerve, I saved your life, you stupid bastard. And you can see me, can't you?"

"Okay, okay, so your idea worked this time. Did the monkeys run away or did they all burn to death?"

"Not too likely they all roasted. Blind though probably. Even if any of them are still able to attack again, we know how to deal with them now—no problem there. We have more than enough signal flares for a repeat performance, if it's needed. What's puzzling me is who carved the masks they wore? And why did they attack us?"

I had read a novel once about ancient civilizations who had trained gorillas to guard their mines. After these societies were destroyed, the gorillas continued to pass on their killing and guarding duties to the next generation and the practice survived for several centuries.

But we had been attacked by monkeys. They weren't supposed to be as smart as gorillas and shouldn't be trainable in the same way. I wanted to ask Liang about this, but he was in such rough shape I doubted he could tell me his own name. Maybe Lao Yang was right and we should abandon this idiot. He was no use at all and probably never would be.

We stayed in that spot for over ten minutes with no sign of the monkeys and began to feel safe at last. Lao Yang found some food in his pack but I waved it away. "Hunger's not my problem, exhaustion is."

I leaned back against my pack and felt drowsiness creep along my body. Just as I was ready to sink into sleep, the tree began to shake again and horrible crashes echoed above us.

"What the hell? We just polished off the monkeys and now Godzilla's coming for us?" I yelled. "Find a hiding place quick!" A black shadow fell past us and a splash of stinking liquid landed right in my face.

Lao Yang was the first to calm down. He raised the torch. "Go see what fell over there, will you?" he asked.

It was a human being, jammed between the bronze branches with his body horribly contorted, staring with wide eyes, his face covered with blood. Broken ribs jutted through his flesh and it didn't take a medical degree to know that he was dead.

"Holy shit. It's Uncle Tai," Lao Yang said. "No wonder there was no trace of him—he was leading the way."

Liang, conscious at last, leaned over and pressed on

Uncle Tai's chest. Blood spurted from the corpse's mouth and nose. "Fell to his death," Liang sighed. "How could he have been so careless?"

I looked at the bones piercing Tai's skin. His body was twisted like a pretzel shape, probably from bouncing off one branch to the next as he fell.

"Look at him," Liang went on. "All the bones in his body are broken. He wouldn't be in this condition unless he fell from three hundred feet or so."

"God damn it," I groaned, "we've only come maybe one hundred feet so far and we're already whipped. How can we possibly climb for another three hundred? Even if we made it to the top of this tree, we'd be so weak that we'd probably end up like Uncle Tai."

"It's not that bad," Lao Yang reassured me. "We can do this." Then he upended Uncle Tai's backpack to see what we could use and my mood lifted in a heartbeat. We had bullets again, some dynamite, flare guns, ropes, and best of all, another flashlight.

"We're all set now," he announced, "and we can't stay here much longer. It's quite possible some of those monkeys survived and are on their way back up to get us. After a little rest we'll head on our way again. After all, we survived an ascent of Mount Taibai and that's over three thousand feet high. It only took us two days—I tell you this is a mere sightseeing excursion for adventurers like us. Just bite the bullet, my friends."

"Listen asshole, I've bitten more bullets than you've misfired in your lifetime, but the one you want me to bite now is going to kill us all. Even if you and I can squeeze out another ounce of energy, Liang is ready to die. We all need to rest long enough to do us some good."

Liang looked at me gratefully and Lao Yang sighed. "Okay, we'll rest but first we have to get rid of Tai's body. I can't relax with him staring at me."

We carefully lifted the corpse from where it rested on the branches. The body was horribly soft with not one bone left unbroken. As we moved him, a stream of blood flowed from his shattered body, rolling along the tree branches and down the narrow trench that had been carved in its trunk.

Liang grabbed the flashlight, pointed its beam into the trench, looked at the branches, and announced, "Gentlemen, I think I may have figured out what this tree was used for."

CHAPTER TWENTY-SIX

BLOOD SACRIFICES

Lao Yang and I were both ready to throw him off the tree when he stopped, shook his head, and smiled modestly. "Of course I'm not really sure. Maybe the bronze tree isn't so important but the trenches on its trunk are. During sacrificial ceremonies, I'm sure they were used to collect the blood of the victims."

He scraped some black residue from the trench; after several thousand years, it was impossible to tell whether this was dried blood or sediment left by rain. He looked at the branches again and said, "You see, there are these troughs under these branches, going all the way down to the carving of the double-bodied serpent. These branches must have a purpose related to blood sacrifices."

"I don't understand. Why do you think this? And how were those sacrifices conducted, do you have any idea?" I asked.

"Although the sacrificial ceremonies in the Western Zhou dynasty weren't as cruel as the ones in the Shang dynasty, both offered humans in their rites. The ceremonies differed only in the way the victims were killed. Sacrifices for the land were made by burying people alive, sacrifices made for the fire god involved burning people to death; for the god of rivers, people were thrown into a stream to drown.

"Just now we saw Uncle Tai's blood flow along the bronze branches and all the way down the trench into the body of the double-bodied serpent, and probably all the way down to the tree's roots. This makes me think this tree was designed and constructed for blood sacrifices, probably to the god of all trees."

As I listened to Liang's theory, I felt disgusted. Our discovery was nothing more than a gigantic killing tool—and a barbaric one. Imagining countless slaves being thrust into these branches upside down and their blood flowing along the trenches, turning the entire bronze tree into a blood column, I felt I was in the presence of an undying evil.

"Let's climb a little faster," I urged my companions. "Otherwise, when Uncle Tai's blood makes it to the bottom, the god of trees might think someone has come to offer him a sacrifice. If he comes out to investigate, he's going to think we're his offerings."

We struggled upward, Lao Yang holding the flashlight and leading the way. The branches were so close together that it was difficult to find a spot where we could place our hands and feet. It was easy to understand why Uncle Tai had fallen from here—one strong puff of wind could send us tumbling after him. All of us were silent, concentrating on our ascent.

As we went higher, I saw changes in the tunnel that surrounded the bronze tree. The walls now held stalactites and other rock formations; it looked as though we'd gone beyond the part excavated by men and were now in the middle of mountain cliffs, which grew closer to us as we climbed onward.

There were many caves within them on either side, shallow caverns that looked as though things moved within them. We were far enough away that this didn't make me uneasy, but I was curious about what might be inside.

I was so absorbed by what I could barely see that I didn't notice that my companions had come to a halt until I bumped into Liang's butt. I looked up and saw more monkeys above us—but these were all dead.

There were dozens of them, bodies so withered that they almost looked like mummies. Their arms and legs were jammed securely into the bronze branches, holding them in place, and they all wore masks that made them appear as though they were staring at us.

The masks were highly polished; they seemed to be made of stone or perhaps even porcelain. There seemed to be no separation between the masks and the monkeys' heads, looking as though they had been welded together.

Liang stopped us. He pointed to a corpse and said, "Wait a minute. There's something strange about these monkeys. Let me take a closer look."

"You're such a pain in the butt, always having to look at something," Lao Yang snapped. "Be careful. In a minute or two those monkeys are going to begin to think there's something strange about you."

Paying no attention, Liang climbed slowly to the monkey that was closest to him. Removing its mask, he peered at its face and said, "This doesn't look like a monkey. This is a human face."

CHAPTER TWENTY-SEVEN

DEADLY DRAGONS

Two dark sockets were all that remained of the corpse's eyes; its mouth gaped open showing its yellowed teeth. They weren't the fangs of a monkey.

Lao Yang froze for a moment and then said, "What's going on here? I thought you said these masked creatures were monkeys but this obviously is a human corpse."

Stuttering, I replied, "I…I don't know either. Just now when I cracked open that mask, I was certain I saw a monkey beneath it, a big one with yellow fur. This… this…I have no idea what to think now."

Liang suddenly waved and slowly rose to his feet, the mask in his hand. He turned it to examine its underside; there was a bolt the size of a fist in the shape of a snail shell, with a small hole just above it, protruding near the dead man's mouth. He held the mask over his own face and said, "It looks as though this man had to keep his mouth perpetually open in order to wear this mask."

"Not very comfortable," Lao Yang responded.

I looked at the gaping mouth of the corpse and asked, "How could he eat or even sleep with his jaws forced open like that? Smash open that bolt and see if there's anything that might explain how a man could wear this mask and still live."

Liang pushed a ballpoint pen into the hole above the bolt and pried at it; the snail shell shattered, revealing something that looked like a crab's leg, attached to a fossilized insect.

"I've never seen anything like this before," he muttered. "Looks like this mask wasn't put on voluntarily, and it seems as though it was made by the same people who cast this bronze tree. See how the lines engraved in the mask are the same as the ones we saw on the tree's double-bodied serpent."

Lao Yang reached for the mask. Studying it intently for a long time, he said, "Who knows how ancient this bug is; it's probably extinct by now. But look—there's only half of its body here. Where's the other half?"

The bug was curled up in the part of the mask which would have covered the corpse's mouth; there was only one spot where the other half of it could be. I peered into the open mouth and there was the missing half of the bug, attached to the tongue, stretching all the way down to the larynx.

Liang's face contorted with horror. "Throw that away right now! Quick! This mask could be alive!" He struck Lao Yang's hand and the mask tumbled into the darkness, hit a bronze branch with a loud, clanging sound, and fell to the ground in pieces.

Startled, Lao Yang almost lost his balance. "Are you crazy? Why would you think that mask could be a living thing?"

Liang coughed, looking remorseful. Scratching his head and frowning, he said, "I'm really ashamed of myself. Why was I so stupid? Why didn't I think about this earlier? I'm such an idiot. No one can be as stupid as I am!"

27. DEADLY DRAGONS

"What kind of bullshit are you spouting now? Why are you an idiot and what does that have to do with the mask? If you have something to say, just say it, won't you?"

"Listen to me. I have to start from the beginning. In ancient times, the ceremonial places of primitive tribes were considered very holy. Not only were they heavily guarded, but special ceremonies called Gu were performed by a chief to protect the spots, and the god who was worshipped there, from outsiders. These Gu ceremonies were very mysterious and held supernatural powers, especially the one that used particular kinds of insects.

"It's possible that the monkeys and human corpses wearing these masks were part of the ancient Gu ceremonies. I've heard of a Gu insect called the Deadly Dragon that could turn a peaceful man into a killer, making whoever harbored it attack anyone who invaded its territory.

"Deadly Dragons breed and multiply inside the bodies they inhabit until their hosts die. Then they cling to a spot like the bolt of this mask and wait for their next victim.

"I'm afraid that's what we just saw in the mask and in the throat of this corpse. I can't prove it without endangering myself but we all saw that insect attached to the corpse and stretching far down its throat. We have to be very careful in this place."

Lao Yang's complexion was the pale green tint of pistachio ice cream and his voice came out in a faint croak. "You make this sound way too terrifying. If the Deadly Dragon did attach itself to us, couldn't we just tear it off our skin? Is there a hidden danger that you haven't told us about yet?"

"All I've heard is Deadly Dragons are very hard to detach once they've sunk their claws into your flesh. My guess is that there are no simple ways to remove one after it's attached to your body. Prevention is the key in this case. Try not to go near these corpses. Don't forget, this is where Uncle Tai plummeted to his death and I don't think a man of his experience would have stumbled without a good reason. Let's be careful."

Lao Yang frowned. He was about to say something, but nothing came out of his mouth and I took advantage of his silence to ask him a question.

"How much longer do you think we'll have to climb? If our ascent continues to be full of these thick branches, we'll die of exhaustion before we ever make it to the top."

"The branches will become sparser the farther up we go. When I first climbed this tree, I only had a small flashlight with me and the light was bad so I never saw these corpses. There weren't any monkeys chasing me either. So now I have no idea of how far we've already climbed. But there's only one way to go—we can't get lost as long as we continue to go up."

"I have a feeling we shouldn't stay here any longer," I said, "so let's climb higher before we continue our discussion. Don't forget that fat guy, Mr. Wang, who was with Uncle Tai and Pockmark—he could very well be climbing above us and we'll be in trouble if he reaches the top first. He could ambush us as we approach, picking us off one by one the minute we came into his rifle sights."

Lao Yang said, "That makes sense. Wait a second. Let me fire off a signal flare and see if there's anything hiding above us." He took out the signal gun and fired a shot up into the air.

The flare flew upward but didn't hit a ceiling. Oh shit, I groaned to myself. This type of bullet could soar as high as six hundred feet—how much farther were we going to have to climb?

The signal flare burst into flame and then began its descent. Lao Yang watched it fall and muttered, "Looks like the fat jerk from Guangdong isn't hiding up there; maybe Uncle Tai was the only one who made it this far. Hey…what are those things over there?"

The signal flare was now only about a hundred feet above us and under its light we could see objects resting in a branch not far away.

"They're faces, staring at us," I gasped.

"No, they aren't," Lao Yang whispered. "Those are more of those damned masks."

CHAPTER TWENTY-EIGHT

IN MIDAIR

As the flare fell closer to them, the masks began to move, trying to get away from the ball of searing flame. From where we sat, they looked like large insect bodies with human faces.

These had to be the Deadly Dragons Liang had just described, taking shelter in the masks which had provided perfect breeding grounds for them.

"Who would think we'd be so lucky that we'd run into these monsters right away? And who could ever imagine there could be so many of them in one place?"

Lao Yang didn't answer, his eyes fixed upon the masks that clung to the tree trunk. Each mask had a different facial expression—some looked as though they were in agony, some seemed racked by sorrow, others glared ferociously, but the worst were the ones with maniacal grins.

Liang had been calm enough when he told us about the masks, but the real thing had him choking for breath. "Oh no," he gasped, "those are Deadly Dragons, alive and dangerous, under those masks. How are we going to get past them? We're doomed."

"Don't panic," Lao Yang barked at him. "Didn't you

see how they reacted to the signal flare? These things are definitely sensitive to light and heat. We'll turn on our flashlights and walk past them very slowly. They won't dare touch us."

I shook my head. "Don't be so sure. The heat and the brightness of the signal flare is a lot more threatening than a flashlight will be. Remember how the monkeys all fled when they saw the signal flares but they only drew back a little when you tried to scare them with your flashlight. That plan isn't going to work."

"So what do you suggest?" Lao Yang asked me. "Do you have something else in mind?"

I said, "I don't have a clear plan but I do have a vague idea that may not worth talking about."

"Spit it out and let us decide if it's worth a try."

I pointed to the cliffs about thirty feet away and said, "It's too dangerous to climb past these things in a direct way; if what Liang told us is true, these insects will try to grab onto us any way they can. We can't force our way through so we have to go around them. Can you think of any way that we could swing to the cliffs on the opposite side? You can see the crevices in them that will make them fairly easy to climb—and we'll be able to take a good, long rest once we're out of this damned tree."

Lao Yang looked at the cliffs and yelled, "That…that far? Swing over there?"

I nodded. "That's the idea. Don't we have ropes? Take them out and see if they're long enough. If not, I guess we can only go back down and come back with a flamethrower next time."

Lao Yang removed the rope that was coiled around

his waist, hung it down the trunk of the tree, and made a rough estimate of the distance it covered. "Not long enough. It wouldn't get us over there even if we tied all our belts to it."

I pulled the rope back up and found it was double-stranded. "It's okay," I said. "We can unbraid the two strands and tie them together. That'll be long enough."

"Are you sure? The rope is as thin as a rice noodle, are you sure it won't snap in two?" Liang asked. "Please don't be reckless."

"Do we have any choice?" I snapped. I separated the strands, tied them together to make one long rope, and handed it to Lao Yang. He took a water bottle from his backpack, tied it to the rope with a sailor's knot to serve as a weight, made a big loop, and flung it toward the cliffs. It fell short on his first three tries, but finally the loop settled around an outcropping of rock. Lao Yang pulled hard, the rope tightened, and the knot held firm.

"All right," Lao Yang shouted, "damn it, it's ready to go, just so long as that rock is stable. Are you sure this is going to work?"

"I don't know," I said, "but I'm ready to give it a try. Unless one of you wants to go first."

They both looked at me in a way that plainly said No way in hell. I sighed like a martyr facing death, patted them both on the back, turned around, and clutched the rope.

The moment my feet left the ground, my nerves were stretched as tight as the rope that I clung to. I closed my eyes, tightened my jaw, and prepared myself to hear the unmistakable death knell of the rope tearing. But it held together, with a slight creaking noise that was very uncomfortable to listen to.

The plunging sensation as the rope soared over empty air was both sickening and thrilling. I forced myself not to look down until the surface of the cliff reached up to grab me and I fell onto solid rock, sobbing like a baby.

"Hey, stop blubbering and look around," Lao Yang shouted. "Is it safe or should you come back over here?"

I looked at the several caves around me. They were all about half my height and were obviously excavated by men, not by nature. Could there be a connection between those who dug these caves and whoever had cast that horrible bronze tree?

The caves were spaced about three or four feet apart. They were empty, as far as I could see, with no visible danger. I waved my hand to signal that it was safe to go ahead with our plan.

Liang was the next to swing his way over and he came to earth even more shaken than I had been. I turned my back to let him regain his equilibrium in peace and watched Lao Yang. He poised himself to swing and then stopped still, his face twisted in a silent shriek.

"Come on!" I shouted but Lao Yang remained motionless, staring at me blankly. He dropped the rope and moved backward, gesturing at me to come back to the tree.

"What the fuck?" I yelled. A voice so quiet that I barely recognized it as Lao Yang's said, "Run for your life. Look up, if you won't listen to me."

On the cliff which had been empty just a moment ago, masks gathered in a huge crowd, surging toward us like a tsunami. The air was filled with a low growling sound;

it had to be coming from the insects that propelled these hellish faces.

How could I be so stupid, I asked myself. There were Deadly Dragons on the tree, so why wouldn't they be on the cliff too? We were finished.

Suddenly there was Lao Yang, beside us on the cliff, holding the rope out to us as he clung to an upper portion of it. Liang and I grabbed it and prepared to soar into the air but our combined weight stretched the rope to its limits. It gave way immediately, sending the three of us tumbling to the very edge of the cliff.

Losing his grip on the rope, Lao Yang began to slip over the brink of the precipice. He grabbed onto a nearby rock and pulled himself to safer ground. My head was bleeding and Liang was a wreck, blubbering and babbling to himself.

As his voice became louder and more hysterical, a Deadly Dragon under a mask heard him and leaped down onto his face, clawing at his flesh. Liang shrieked and tried to protect his face with both hands but the mask was already in place, completely covering his face. He tried to claw it away but it seemed glued to his skin.

I clambered over the rocks to help him but a large black shadow dropped from the sky and began to grip at my own face. I could see nothing at all as the mask dropped into place but I could feel hairy, slender tentacles trying to force their way into my mouth.

In a panic, I clutched at the rocks with one hand and used the other to try to pull away the mask. Clamping my teeth together tightly, I kept the tentacles from coming inside my mouth. I yanked hard and the mask fell away, landing right beside Lao Yang. He cursed viciously as he smashed it to pieces with his flashlight.

I exhaled at last but when I turned around, four more Deadly Dragons were coming toward my head. I found my gun and fired but another ten came in their place.

Lao Yang and I began to move away toward the edge of the cliff but we were stopped by the sound of screams and sobs. Looking up, we saw Liang, his body covered with Deadly Dragons. He cried and struggled as he tried to shake them off, but for every one that he managed to remove, ten more came in its place.

I kept shooting as I retreated until I ran out of bullets, but that didn't help; the Deadly Dragons surrounded us on all sides like an electric fence. The surrounding cliffs were covered with them, and their strange eerie growl echoed in my head. The sound was so compelling it crowded everything from my brain, distracting me from protecting myself. The bugs knew it and swarmed toward my face; I forced myself back to the business of warding them off.

There was no way to escape these monstrous insects. They had us trapped. Lao Yang opened fire and that frightened away a few of them, shattering several of the masks to bits. But in less than a second, another flock had arrived as replacements. Lao Yang stopped shooting, took off his shirt, and wrapped it around his face, yelling, "Quick! Cover your face and then go get your flashlight—I'll keep you covered."

I looked and saw my flashlight, still beaming where I had placed it. No Deadly Dragons were anywhere near it; they seemed to be afraid of it. But between me and the light, hordes of them swarmed, separating me from the flashlight.

"Impossible," I shouted back to Lao Yang. "You do it and I'll cover you instead."

"I'm the one holding the gun—just do it and shut up!" Lao Yang screamed.

I looked at the bugs and almost puked. There were so many of them, all protected by the masks.

Lao Yang started to throw a string of curses at me for being slow but suddenly his voice changed from anger to perplexity. "What's going on with you anyway? How are you doing that?"

"What the hell do you mean? If you think you have time to fart, then let it out. "

"Take a look at yourself; there's not one of those damned bugs anywhere on your body. How is that possible?"

I lowered my head and saw that Lao Yang was right. He and Liang were covered with Deadly Dragons, which they couldn't shake off no matter how hard they struggled. But on my body there were none at all.

I immediately realized that except for the few that had flown at my face a moment ago, no others had attacked me. I'd been so frightened that I hadn't noticed that there were no threats as far as I was concerned. Now I saw that although the Deadly Dragons crawled in my direction, as soon as they came close they veered off on another course. It really looked as though they might be afraid of me.

What's going on? I thought to myself, and lifted my arm to see if I could grab one. Before I could, the entire horde of Deadly Dragons rushed away from where I sat.

"Fuck me—that's incredible. Is there something on your hand that repels them? Take a look—and hurry!"

I checked my hands. Except for the smears of blood and dirt, there was nothing on them.

That was strange. What were they afraid of?

As I watched them retreat, I remembered when Poker-face had dripped his blood into the water to frighten away the corpse-eaters in the cavern of the blood zombies.

Holy shit, I thought, staring at my hands, could it be my blood? How could the blood of an ordinary guy like me frighten monsters like the Deadly Dragons? My mind felt as though it were made of mud; all I could do was stare and wonder.

"Give me a hand here, damn it," Lao Yang yelled, and I reached over to pull him in my direction. Like cockroaches faced with a cloud of poison, the Deadly Dragons that clung to his flesh dropped to the ground and scuttled off, just the way the corpse-eaters had retreated when they encountered Poker-face's blood.

I raised my arm and climbed a few steps toward Liang, who was writhing in agony. I drew near him and the bugs shrank backward, their growls turning into terrified squeaks as they rushed away.

Stunned by what he saw, Lao Yang stared at me as if I were a monster. I ignored him and put my hands on Liang's face, and the mask that clung to his skin immediately curled away from my fingers. I grabbed it and ripped it off, and a long, fleshy object covered with mucus came with it, emerging from Liang's throat. When Liang saw what had been in his mouth, he gagged and covered himself with vomit.

The Deadly Dragon struggled violently in my hand, and I almost lost my grip. It was so disgusting that I couldn't bear to hold it so I smashed it against a rock. A green fluid gushed from its body, covering my hand.

The Deadly Dragons had retreated but didn't go very far; they continued to surround us, but their circle got smaller by the minute. Liang began to come back to his senses and Lao Yang gathered up the rope, the water bottle, and my flashlight. "What we really need is still on that damned tree. Somehow we have to get our food and gear if we're going to survive," he said.

"First of all we have to get some rest or we'll go crazy," I told him.

"No, first of all we need to know how you suddenly became our hero. Why didn't you ward the bugs off earlier so we didn't have to go through that hell?"

"I don't have a fucking clue. It's all like a dream—or a nightmare."

Lao Yang took a look at the blood on my hand, touched it lightly, and sniffed at it. He asked, "On the way over here, did you touch anything special with your hands? Think about it carefully…looks like you discovered an antidote to these damned bugs and never realized it."

I thought for a moment. The other guys had touched everything that I had. The only thing that they didn't touch was my blood, but that didn't make any sense. If my blood was that powerful, I would've made a huge difference during other dangerous times—in the cavern of the blood zombies or within the undersea tomb. If it really was my blood that had just saved us, then why wasn't it powerful before? Could it have been that when I touched Poker-face's blood as it dripped into the cavern's pool, its power came to me, but in a delayed fashion? Crazy, I told myself, this is all impossible.

"What are you talking about, you two?" Liang had seen nothing that had just happened since his eyes had been covered by the mask.

"You don't know," Lao Yang told him, "but this guy saved us all. It happened like this..."

Liang was silent until he heard the whole story and then turned to me, gesturing with both hands. "Have you ever in your life eaten something that was black and flat and about this size?"

CHAPTER TWENTY-NINE

QILIN

Liang touched the blood on one of my hands, smelled it, and said to me, "When I listened to what Lao Yang said just now, I remembered something. Once an old gentleman told me there was something that, if eaten, would give a man's blood the power to ward off evil. The fact that those insects didn't come close to you makes me think you may have consumed this without realizing it or comprehending the power it would bring you. Think about it. Have you ever eaten something black and about this size, something flat and thin?"

"I have no idea. Everything that I've eaten recently has been gobbled down in a hurry. I haven't had time to pay attention to what I've been eating lately, what with everything else that's been going on here."

Lao Yang laughed. "I've only heard that the blood of a black dog or rooster can ward off evil. What a surprise that our old friend here has this talent. Don't tell anyone about it. Otherwise, everyone's going to want some of your blood and in a few days you'll be drained dry!" He laughed again, then winced in pain.

I ignored him; we were all in bad shape at this point. I asked Liang, "Can you give me a more specific description?

There are so many things that are black and flat."

Liang thought for a while and said with some embarrassment, "I've never seen it myself. I've only heard other people's descriptions, a long time ago. I'm afraid I can't be helpful at all."

"Too bad," I sighed.

Liang smiled and said, "Don't let it bother you. This isn't a bad thing. If it weren't for you, we'd all be dead by now. Look at it this way; now that you have this gift, everything will be easy for you when you rob graves in the future."

"We won't know if it was because of me that we're safe until I have my blood tested. We could still be in trouble. Let's take advantage of this lucky break and hurry out of here. We can talk again when we're safe."

Liang was ready to take a rest again, but when he saw the insects lurking in the background waiting to make more trouble, he agreed with me. We set off on our climb, but after a few steps, Lao Yang suddenly grabbed my hand and pulled me to a stop. "Wait…wait a second!"

I turned around and saw that his face was pale and sweaty; he looked sick. "What's wrong?" I asked.

Lao Yang held onto a rock with one hand and touched his back with another. He grimaced and said, "I don't know what's going on; I felt a stabbing pain a moment ago when I laughed. I might have hurt my back when the rope broke and I smashed into the rocks. Can you take a look for me and see if there's anything wrong? I don't have the strength to look for myself."

"Stand still," I told him and looked at his back. There was a small bruised indentation near one of his ribs. I pressed on it and Lao Yang squealed like a pig at a slaughterhouse.

He doubled over and almost knocked me down. Whatever was wrong, it was a serious injury—maybe a broken rib.

"How bad does it look?" Lao Yang gasped.

"Hard to tell just from looking but I know you can't make this climb. Let's find a flat spot on the ground and take a closer look at that back of yours."

"Forget it," he argued, "we don't have any time to waste. Our flashlight's going to go out soon and then we'll be in deep shit. Keep moving."

Liang took a look at the bruise, shook his head, and said, "Don't be silly. We have to take a look. If you have a fracture, then we have to take care of it right away. Otherwise, the bone could pierce your lung, and then you'll be finished. I have a little bit of knowledge about this sort of thing and we're not far from the top right now. We can afford a slight delay."

Lao Yang was ready to keep arguing, but it was too painful for him to speak. I noticed that the small caves nearby looked as though they had flat interior surfaces and I gestured to Liang. Without a word, the two of us picked up Lao Yang and carried him into one of the caves.

I checked the area again to see if there was any immediate danger while Liang turned our rifle into a splint, tying it with ropes to Lao Yang's back. "What do you think the problem is?" I asked. He lowered his voice as he replied, "I don't think there are any broken bones but there could be a crack or two. I can help him so he won't hurt so much but you'd better try and persuade him not to do any more climbing. He's in no shape for that."

I looked Liang straight in the eye and knew there was a hidden message beneath his words. He was trying to persuade me to retreat rather than go further, which he had already done more than once.

I knew he was a coward, and only Lao Yang's bullying had kept him from voicing his objections directly. Now that there was a ready-made excuse, of course he was going to take advantage of it. Who knew if he was telling the truth about the extent of Lao Yang's injury?

Sensing my suspicion, Liang quickly followed up his suggestion. "We're not stupid men, any of us, and we know the risks we continue to face. Do you want to die on these cliffs—and for what? Treasures that may not even exist?"

I glanced at Lao Yang, who was in so much pain that he was paying no attention to our conversation. "Go take a rest," I told Liang quietly. "We'll talk about this when we've replenished our energy; we're all too tired to think right now."

Liang muttered something inaudible, lay down near the far side of the cave, rubbed his bruises, and was silent. I sat down myself, massaging my aching temples, and began to think carefully about Liang's words.

We had come too far to give up now, I was convinced, but on the other hand, Liang's argument made sense. Lao Yang was out of commission, Liang was a weakling in every sense of the word, except for his brain, and I was exhausted almost beyond all measure. To continue our ascent would be suicidal, although I knew Lao Yang would never agree with me.

I could imagine his shouting. "You're siding with that wimpy bastard instead of one of your oldest friends? How do you know this jerk isn't working against us so his associates can get to the treasure before we do? Get a fucking grip on yourself and keep going—I certainly am."

There was no easy solution, I decided. We could only work out a plan one step at a time. I looked at my companions; they were both asleep and soon so was I.

When I woke up, I felt completely restored. Sticking my head out of the cave entrance, I felt even better when I saw only a few of the Deadly Dragons hanging around. Turning on my flashlight, I looked upward and could see the top of the cliff. It looked as though it would only be a three- or four-hour climb to reach it—how could we turn back now?

Lao Yang was still snoring, and I turned to check on Liang. His spot in the cave was empty and he was nowhere to be seen. The rifle that served as a splint for Lao Yang had disappeared and when I looked at my belt, I realized my pistol was gone too.

"Son of a bitch!" I yelled. "How could that little coward get away with this?" But why didn't he steal the flashlight too? How could he find his way through the darkness? It would be an easy matter to catch up with him, especially since he was such a slow-moving little bastard.

Just as I stepped out of the cave, a shadow swung down from above and kicked me square in my chest. Breathless, I fell to the ground; struggling to get to my feet, I felt a fist land on my chin. Standing before me was a fat guy with a rifle in one hand, cigarette in the other.

I knew who this was; it was the guy from the south, Mr. Wang. Pointing the rifle at my belly, he forced me against the outer wall of the cave. Then he turned to that sniveling little coward, Liang, who was slinking behind him.

"Is this the guy who ate Qilin sanguis and now has its power?"

CHAPTER THIRTY

BETRAYED BY A RAT

Liang jerked his chin in my direction dismissively and nodded. You asshole, I thought, I was the one who defended you and rescued you, and now you stab me in the back. Why in hell didn't I let you die, you miserable little rat?

Mr. Wang took a lantern from his backpack, lit it, and set it on the ground. It was expensive, designed for high-altitude, snowy terrain, and it gave off heat as well as light. Then he took some packs of crackers from his pocket and threw them at me, his rifle still pointed at my belly.

What the fuck is going on here, I thought as I picked up the packs and tossed them back at his feet. "Don't bother feeding me if you plan to kill me; just do it now, damn you."

Liang grinned, turned to Wang, and said, "I told you, he's completely naïve—he has no clue about what's really going on here."

Wang shook his head and tossed the food to me again. "Look, if I give you something to eat, that means I'm not going to kill you. But you're lucky. With your attitude, you'd be dead if you ever run into a guy with a bad temper."

He was right; he was completely different from Uncle Tai, who would have killed me without a second's thought. Wang seemed to be a really nice guy, except he had just kicked the shit out of me and was still holding a rifle close to my stomach. He wasn't that easy to figure out.

As if he could sense my confusion, Mr. Wang took a long drag on his cigarette and continued. "I'm not like Old Tai or the other guys. I'm a businessman and in my world there are no permanent relationships. Neither friends nor enemies are set in stone."

Liang said, "Mr. Wang, why don't you just come out and say what's going on? This guy is fairly intelligent when faced with facts but I warn you, that sleeping lout is another story. The only person he'll listen to is his friend here."

Wang laughed, turned to me, and said, "All right. I'll be straight with you. I'm a merchant and I don't like violence. You know for yourself that before I came into the picture you were in deep shit. This is dangerous territory and getting out of it alive is no easy matter. Tai and his brainless nephew are already dead. I don't need to kill you; you'll die if you don't join forces with me. But if you do, you have nothing to lose; you'll come out of here richer than when you came in."

Seeing that I didn't react to his words, he handed me a cigarette and added, "It's no problem at all if you don't want to come with us. I'll give you some gear and you can go back down on your own. But you've got an injured man with you. How are you going to manage with him?"

He had a point; I was almost ready to agree to his offer. Still, something didn't measure up. He had weapons and equipment and knowledge. Why did he need me and how could I trust him? Look at the way his little flunky Liang had treated us.

As these thoughts flashed across my mind, I decided to join Wang now and think about a better course of action later. With Lao Yang in such bad shape, I really had no other choice. My big advantage here was that Wang was underestimating me, just as I had that slimy little creep Liang, who now had the upper hand. It wasn't impossible that I could accomplish that same role reversal myself somewhere down the line or at least take back our guns.

Meekly and with some hesitation, I asked, "What do you want me to do? Tell me, so I can help in any way I can."

Mr. Wang grinned and Liang patted me on the shoulder, as he shifted back to his old self again. "Wise decision, young man. You're one of us now and I can finally tell you everything. But it's a long story so let's talk about it over a meal."

I could have strangled the filthy little hypocrite if Wang weren't still pointing his rifle at me, but instead I smiled. "I can't wait to hear what you have to say."

Liang gazed over at the bronze tree. "It all began with this tree, which was first discovered thousands of years ago when a worker on this mountain discovered a bronze column while digging a mine shaft. He could see neither top nor bottom to it and was sure it ran all the way down to the base of the peak and all the way up to the summit. His discovery upset the local community, who said the column was sacred. Some said if people tried to dig it up, the deeper it would sink itself into the earth, so the root would never be found. Others claimed it was the handle of the ax that the god Pangu had used to create the sky—anyone who dug it up would find the sacred ax. Feng Shui masters said it was a nail that had been hammered into the earth twelve hundred miles deep to keep a mythical dragon from flying away. If the column were ever dug up, China would be in desperate peril.

"Not long after this discovery an army of deaf-mute soldiers received secret orders to march to Mount Taibai to investigate the column. None of them returned, disappearing without a trace. Another battalion of the same "Silent Army" was sent four months later. They found the column and occupied Mount Taibai, closing it off to the public. They continued the excavation using the forced labor of three thousand prisoners.

"When the excavation had been underway for a little over four years, the prisoners had made their way up to the caves where we stand now and all the way down to the bottom of the mountain without unearthing the root of the bronze tree. In the process they unearthed a stone box carved with the figures of dragons. When they moved it, they could feel something shift inside but they found it was impossible to open. Not wanting to damage it beyond repair, they sent it to the emperor.

"Soon after this the emperor rewarded everyone who worked on the excavation project and the soldiers had a party to celebrate. Drunk, they challenged each other to climb the bronze tree, making wagers as to who would be the first to get to the top. Nobody knows now what the outcome of this had been. All that was recorded from this point was that they were ordered to build a boardwalk so the emperor would have a safe viewing area when he came to see the tree for himself. And finally we're told the project claimed so many lives that it was never completed."

When Liang reached the end of his story, we all left the cave and Mr. Wang handed me a pair of binoculars. By the light of the lantern that he held, I could see a portion of a boardwalk spiraling up the cliff, not too far above us.

"If we can get to that boardwalk, it will save us a lot of time and energy," he remarked, "but I doubt that will be as easy as it sounds. Now our friend Liang here is a scholar, fine for research and academic pursuits, but no use in any sort of battle, as you probably have found out already. That's why I need you and your friend to come with us."

It was hard for me to tell, even with binoculars, what sort of shape the boardwalk was in. It sure as hell would be different from the boardwalk we had walked along in the park. "It's going to be a miracle if much of this boardwalk is left at all," I said, "and what remains is probably none too sturdy. What makes you think it's going to be useful to us?"

"This was built for the royal journey of an emperor, not as a temporary path for workers, so its construction was of the highest standard possible. Many ancient structures from that period of history are still solid and strong today, so I don't see that this will be any different. If we do find any deterioration we have a lot of rope to use in scaling the cliff wall, and if we have to climb, even a fragment of this boardwalk will make things easier for us."

Wang spoke with a tone that left no room for argument so I swallowed a few choice words and fell silent. "Rest for fifteen minutes or so," he told me. "Then I'll go with you to the boardwalk while Liang stays with your friend."

I sat quietly while Wang and Liang talked together in Cantonese. I understood enough to know that they were talking about Qilin sanguis, which was still a mystery to me. Since we were a team now, or at least so they thought, I broke in, "Liang, what is this Qilin sanguis anyway? Will it hurt me? Is it dangerous?"

"Don't worry," Liang assured me. "It's only a blood clot formed when the blood of a qilin thickens. It's a rare and costly medicine, but it isn't really made from the blood of a qilin, that special, magical deer that holds great powers. It comes from the sap of a plant called the qilin blood vine, usually only found in the south. Although it's usually used for common medical purposes, at one time it was used to smoke dead bodies. Some people also used to press a piece of this against a corpse's navel before burying the body; the corpse would rot away but wouldn't be consumed by maggots.

"As it aged, this medicine would change color, from dark red to black, becoming progressively darker as time went on. At a certain point, its texture changed and when put in a person's mouth, it would dissolve. Then insects would no longer plague whoever had eaten it, not even mosquitoes in the summer.

"I always thought this was only a legend until I heard what had happened with you and the Deadly Dragons. I've never heard of this having any side effects but if you're going to worry about something, save your concern for the Deadly Dragons themselves. Who knows what those things are fully capable of? You and your buddy have got to be careful as we go farther up the mountain."

Lao Yang still was dead to the world as I got ready to go up to the boardwalk with Mr. Wang. It was farther away than it looked and it took us half an hour to reach it. Mr. Wang was right: it was in great condition, supported by a framework of bamboo poles that was impervious to moisture and made soft, whooshing, almost comforting sounds when we walked over it.

As we climbed, our route was obstructed by vines and the roots of banyan trees, blocking the path like octopus tentacles. We hacked our way through them with machetes that Mr. Wang carried. The tree roots had cracked through the rocks above us and they tumbled in our path with alarming regularity. We had to cope with what was underfoot as well as with what was overhead, which made this more exhausting and stressful than any previous ascents.

Focused on our trek, we had no idea of how far we had come and trudged steadily onward until a large hole appeared before us. It was a gap that was easily thirty feet across, probably caused by boulders falling from above. I estimated the width of this obstacle and told Mr. Wang, "There's no way we're crossing this without using a rope."

When we checked the time, we found we'd been hiking for an hour but looking down at the spot where we began made us realize how short a distance we had come. "We're not going to make it to the top in an hour," Wang said. "We're already worn out and we need a rest. Our clothes are soaked with sweat and if we don't dry them out we're going to get sick."

We found a cave near the boardwalk; it was covered with tree roots and the inside was dry. Mr. Wang took out his lantern and it soon emitted its miraculous heat and blazing light. We hung our clothes so they would dry and had a snack as Mr. Wang pointed his flashlight in the direction of the bronze tree. After scrutinizing it for several minutes he said, "Come over here and look at this. You can see the top of the tree here but what's that other thing farther up?"

I picked up the binoculars and saw something wrapped in a mass of roots but was unable to tell what it might be.

The boardwalk that we followed up the walls of the cave went farther than I'd thought, extending above the bronze treetop. Had the tree sunk over the years so its height dropped below the boardwalk? Were the roots we saw those of the same sort of gigantic banyan trees that we'd encountered earlier? Twisted together like the pale hands of ghosts, the roots seemed to grip the bronze tree trunk as though trying to pull it straight up from the deepest reaches of hell. It was an eerie sight and suddenly I wished I were anywhere else but where I was at the moment.

"You see how thick the roots are here?" Mr. Wang asked. "That means this is near the topsoil and that this is a natural cave, not man-made. When people came in ancient times to perform their ceremonies of worship, it would have been impossible for them to dig their way through the mountain. They had to have come here through the tunnel of a cave, which will lead us back to the outside world, once we find the route. Maybe we won't need to retrace our steps to get off this mountain."

Oh sure, I thought. I know all too well that natural caves aren't necessarily tranquil refuges of safety. There could well be things we'd encounter there that would force us to make other plans on the spur of the moment. Suddenly I was jolted as Mr. Wang gave me a little shove.

"Look at that mass of roots over there," he pointed. "It looks as though it's holding a bronze statue but I can't see it clearly. Let's get closer for a better look."

Looking in the direction he pointed toward, I saw what looked like two bronze arms in the tangle of roots just below the top of the tree trunk. A chill of recognition passed over me. "That looks a lot like the statue we saw when we entered the Gate to Hell," I said. "Does this mean we're near the end of our search?"

CHAPTER THIRTY-ONE

SAME OLD STORY

We decided we'd scale the cliff to get past the gaping hole in the boardwalk and closer to the statue. The tree roots that shrouded the slopes would make the climb easy and if we fell we'd land on the boardwalk. Knowing I wouldn't plunge to my death made me feel a little less apprehensive.

Mr. Wang swiftly scaled the cliff with his pickax while I secretly hoped he would fall. But he was surprisingly expert in spite of his corpulence and was soon on a higher and less dilapidated part of the boardwalk. He turned, threw the pickax down for me to use, and then ran off toward the statue. I climbed cautiously and slowly, and was only halfway up when I heard Wang call, "Come here at once! I think there's more than one statue in these roots. And there's something else carved here—I can't make out what it is."

Clutching a rocklike root, I swung myself up and then onto the boardwalk. I could see Mr. Wang's flashlight bobbing up ahead, three levels above where I stood. Panting, I joined him and he handed me the binoculars.

"Hell," I mumbled, "there are as many arms as an octopus's in that clump of roots, and they're placed in all four directions. I can't tell if they're all the same size or shape—can you? But it's plain to see that they're huge."

We kept going along the boardwalk, getting closer to the top of the bronze tree. We could see a worship platform beyond the crown of the tree, with four statues standing on it, one in each corner.

Mr. Wang stopped, looked around, then turned to me and said, "I think there must be something in the middle of the platform. We have to get over there and take a look." He folded the pointed edge of his pickax into a curved shape and tied it to a rope to turn it into a grappling hook. Like a cowboy, he swung it a few times in the air above his head and hurled it toward the platform.

The pickax hooked onto a root near the worship platform, wrapped around the root a few times, and fortunately hooked right back onto the rope. Wang pulled the rope so taut that the tree root shook a little and a crowd of strange-looking grey insects emerged from the cracks in the root and rapidly scurried away.

Mr. Wang frowned. "You go first this time!"

I knew he was afraid; I silently called him a few choice names and said a couple of rude things about his mother, while measuring the distance with my eyes. It was nothing compared to other hazards this mountain had already thrown at me. I nodded and climbed onto the rope, which I realized, with reluctant appreciation, Wang had thrown perfectly. With very little effort, I made my way to the other side.

"Check out those damned bugs," Mr. Wang yelled.

"They're not Deadly Dragons," I called back. "I'm sure they're harmless. It's okay. Most of them are gone."

He came across and we began to explore our surroundings. The roots here were almost as thick as two or three of my thighs put together. They were all connected in a confusing maze that somehow felt evil, as though they were determined to catch us and keep us there forever. "Banyan trees," Mr. Wang observed, "I've never liked them."

The tangle of roots enveloped everything in sight; it was impossible to see what was in their clutches. We did our best to clear them away with our machetes but their rocklike surfaces made that impossible.

"There are some hollow spots between these roots—I can see them," Mr. Wang said. "Let's split up and check the openings one by one for a clear viewing spot." I hesitated, thinking this wasn't a plan that would do us any good, but he gestured at me impatiently. "Go," he snapped.

Somehow I knew this was a very violent man, despite his protests to the contrary. He reminded me a bit of Fats. They even had the same surname; could they somehow be related? No, I thought, Fats is kind and he always says what's on his mind. Mr. Wang never does.

The roots that coiled everywhere made the area look like a burial mound. In spite of our combined efforts, we could find no place where we could see through the tangles. My back ached and I felt miserable. What did Mr. Wang think he was going to accomplish in his stubborn quest? Why did Lao Yang insist on coming here, and where was he when I needed him?

As I grumbled to myself, Mr. Wang jabbed me in the ribs, then held his finger to his lips in a hushing gesture. He waved his hand and pulled me down to where he squatted, cupping his hand to his ear. We both listened. From within the mass of twisted roots came a clicking sound, low and regular, like teeth chattering in the cold.

"These sounds have the same regular cadence as a monk tapping on a wooden drum. It sounds almost mechanical. There's something in here—but who knows if it's living or dead," Mr. Wang whispered.

Then he raised his rifle, pulled the bolt, and signaled to me to follow him. Together we crept up to where the sounds were coming from, at the edge of a hole in the middle of a mass of roots. Mr. Wang turned on his flashlight and pointed it into the opening. The sounds stopped.

He glanced at me and whispered, "We have to go in there now."

I frowned and said, "Let's give this some thought. Don't you think it might be dangerous?"

He nodded. "Yes. We can't both go at the same time. One of us will go down first to find the path."

It didn't take a spectacular feat of mental energy to know which of us would go first. Mr. Wang saw the look on my face, pointed his rifle toward me, and explained, "I'm too fat. You go; I'll be right behind you. Don't worry. Nothing will happen to you." He pushed me toward the opening.

I looked down into blackness. I turned and saw the rifle barrel. I had no choice. As I began to scramble into the opening, Mr. Wang handed me a walkie-talkie. "Once you get deep inside, use this to tell me what you find. You're a lucky man to have this opportunity, you know."

"Mr. Wang. Let's be honest with each other. This walkie-talkie isn't going to be enough. I'm risking my life for you. If I die in there, there'll be nobody left to help you. If I can't have a gun, at least allow me a blade, okay?"

Mr. Wang shrugged, drew a small dagger from his waistband, and tossed it to me. It was no more than a hunting knife but it was better than nothing at all. Clutching it tightly, I crawled down into the opening.

It was a long tunnel, damp and musty, its walls covered with mushrooms. The grey insects we had seen earlier were everywhere here and scurried away as I approached. The tunnel forked off in several directions. "Shit," I muttered, "which way should I go?"

As I peered around I saw that one of the forks had been marked, and I felt relieved that I wasn't the first man to enter this place. I clambered along in that direction until I reached an empty, hollow spot; it was a small, cavernous chamber. In one corner I could see a piece of slate; as I came closer I saw it was the edge of a stone coffin placed on a burial platform.

On my hands and knees, I managed to get close to the coffin, which was in a very tight space. Carved on its cover was the same double-bodied serpent that was engraved upon the bronze tree.

My walkie-talkie crackled with Mr. Wang's angry voice. "Where the hell are you? What's going on? Have you found anything?"

"There's a coffin here!" I replied. "It had to have been sheer hell to get it down in this place. It's in such a confined space I can't even sit up, let alone stand. Nobody but the man who cast the bronze tree could have been important enough to be buried here."

Then I stopped talking. The coffin wasn't sealed; the cover was raised where a tree root had snaked its way inside. "Mr. Wang," I croaked, forcing out my words, "this coffin is open."

I crawled to the spot where the cover was raised and pointed my flashlight inside. The interior was grey and empty.

I picked up my walkie-talkie. "The coffin is empty and I have no idea what it might have once contained. But maybe your flashlight's much stronger than mine; maybe you can get a better look. Come on down. It's safe enough." Except, I thought, for me. The minute I can see your head, I'm going to cut your throat.

The only sound that came over the walkie-talkie was a lot of static. "Mr. Wang?" I called. Again only static replied, followed by an explosive thunderclap that echoed through my ears. Then over the airwaves came the sound of violent sobbing.

CHAPTER THIRTY-TWO

A FOG IN THE COFFIN

There I was, alone in a cramped little space, lying beside a coffin, with a horrible sobbing sound coming from my only link to the world outside. A shaky voice began to chant something incomprehensible; I turned down the volume immediately and tried to stay calm. I turned the walkie-talkie on and off several times and listened again.

The eerie sounds were gone but static still blurted occasionally, as though Mr. Wang might be calling me. I adjusted the frequency and shouted into the radio but there was no reply. This has to be some sort of electrical interference, I reassured myself, maybe sunspots, although that seemed unlikely considering that I was underground. What could be causing this and how could I make it go away?

I crawled around the cave, looking for a spot with good reception, and found that the closer I was to the coffin, the louder the noises were. When I moved away, the interference was weaker. Strange, I thought, could the noises be caused by something inside the coffin?

Cautiously, I lowered the walkie-talkie into the coffin and instantly the static became a bloodcurdling scream. I pulled it out quickly, shaking so badly I almost lost my grip on it.

Shit, I thought, there's something in this coffin that produces irregular electromagnetic waves. Is this a natural occurrence or something more bizarre? I had read once that in a place where there had been a massacre, or near a large burial ground, an omnipresent wave of electromagnetic interference had been detected more than once. Some said that this was generated by the energy of the decomposing corpses, while others said they were messages being sent by a large number of spirits. Could there be a strong electromagnetic wave transmitted by a body or a spirit inside this coffin?

Under the dim beam of my flashlight, the roots that surrounded me looked like the deformed skeletons of snakes, and the noises that emerged from the walkie-talkie made me feel as though something in the coffin was inviting me to come and join it. I had just enough sense left to turn the damned thing off.

I felt dizzy and my vision began to blur. I began to gasp for air and suddenly I felt very, very cold. I could vaguely hear a voice that sounded like Mr. Wang, muffled and faint as though it were filtered through ten layers of quilts. Just a short time before, I'd plotted Wang's murder; now my only thought was that my own death seemed uncomfortably close. How could I get out of this horrible space before it killed me? And then I heard that clicking sound again, like chattering teeth, uncomfortably nearby. It sounded as though it came from the coffin.

I pulled out my hunting knife and crawled toward the coffin, but as I approached, the noise stopped. The sudden silence was as terrifying as the clicking sound had been. My body stiffened with fear as something grabbed my shoulder.

I turned and stabbed wildly; my flashlight struck one of the roots and went out, leaving me in absolute darkness. Something caught my hand and pulled me backward as a voice yelled, "Stop struggling, you damned fool."

The beam of a strong flashlight blinded me and then I saw Mr. Wang. His fist was drawn back, and then it rocketed against my face full force. "Are you fucking with me, you stupid bastard? What have you been doing down here while I was calling you? Are you trying to double-cross me or murder me?"

I tried to explain what had been going on but he was too enraged to listen, striking me again so hard that my ears buzzed. "You maniac," I screamed and rammed my head into his chest as hard as I could. We wrestled our way across the cavern floor, Wang trying to get a stranglehold on my throat, me writhing in my attempts to kick him in the groin.

As we fought, I saw he had dropped his flashlight. I reached out for it, grabbed it, and smashed it against his head. He slumped to one side and in my triumph, I forgot there was no room to stand in this cave. I pulled myself to my feet, groping for the knife in my belt, and hit my head hard against the roof of the cavern. I fell to the ground just as Wang regained his senses; he came at me with a dagger in his hand and death in his eyes.

Picking up the flashlight again, I directed its beam squarely into Wang's face but he kept coming, swiping the knife at my jugular. He missed. I grabbed his arm with my free hand, just as the flashlight went out. In the unexpected darkness, he stopped moving and I bashed him again with the heavy light.

The impact of the blow turned the flashlight on again and I saw Wang, lying on the ground, his mouth bleeding. He looked unconscious but I knew better than to be taken in by him again. I kicked his body closer to the coffin, knowing that if he were conscious, he wouldn't be able to keep from moving away from it. He remained motionless.

Rapidly I rolled him up and into the opening where the tree root kept the coffin cover from closing. His legs went through easily but the rest of his fat body was stuck. With a final kick, I managed to push him into the coffin. "There, you son of a bitch, rest easy," I gasped.

Before I could move away, Wang's arm emerged from the coffin and grabbed my leg, pulling me in with him. I tried to grab at something to forestall his attack but there was nothing within reach. Wang and I were together within the tomb.

I had thought this coffin was small but I was wrong. It was deep, and I fell at least twelve feet down, landing with a heavy and painful impact. Wang no longer gripped me and I turned on the flashlight that I still had in my grasp. All I could see was a thick, grey mist.

I stood up and swung the flashlight around but saw nothing. Where the hell was Wang? And how could there be such a heavy mist inside a coffin? I stretched out my arm and drops of moisture immediately clung to it.

Since I couldn't see a thing, I didn't dare move forward. Could I climb back up to the coffin lid? I looked up but all I could see were tree roots, stretching down toward me like strands of ivy, all of them covered with odd little pieces of fungus that were soft and slippery to the touch.

On the wall were some bas-relief carvings, unobscured

by the roots, figures that resembled the four statues we had seen outside. It looked as though they were workers who were constructing the bronze tree, all of them wearing clothes that I had seen in pictures of ancient tribal minorities. They were involved in casting sections of tree trunk that now combined to form the spectacular work of art that stood in one piece.

There were many bas-reliefs surrounding me but I was too frightened to take the time to examine them all. As I stood in the mist, I wanted nothing more than to get the hell out of this place. Trying not to panic, I began to work my way up one of the tree roots, but the slippery fungal growth that covered it was like a blanket of ice, glassy and slick. Perhaps I could use my knife as a climbing ax, I thought, or I could shave away the covering of fungus. And then I heard it, that rhythmical clicking sound again, but this time it was behind me, and very, very close by.

CHAPTER THIRTY-THREE

SNEAK ATTACK

The clicking wasn't loud but claimed my attention as though it were rolls of thunder, each one making my entire body flinch. It sounded as though whatever was making the noise was less than three feet away, close enough to reach out and tap me on the back. It was like having my body next to a door while someone tapped on it incessantly, particularly if the creature tapping near me was a ghost.

I couldn't move; I wanted to scream and bit my tongue to keep my mouth from opening. Stop it, I thought, you have no choice but to calm down and face whatever is frightening you—or die in a state of panic. I took a deep breath, gripped my hunting knife, and slowly turned around.

The clicking stopped; there was nothing there but grey mist. A weird rush of air whooshed past me and then was gone. I gulped and made myself direct the rays of my flashlight into the swirls of fog—nothing emerged from the sodden air. Had I imagined the noises? Was oxygen deprivation affecting my brain?

A figure rocketed out from the fog, just missing me, and then disappeared once more. Its shape was massive but moved with amazing speed. "Damn you, Mr. Wang," I spat into the darkness, "stop playing games and come out to face me, you fat coward." I directed my flashlight toward the blade of my knife, making it flash menacingly, hoping the sight of it would cut through the blanket of fog.

He was probably hiding, waiting for me to come closer so he could strike without any effort or risk on his part, the sneaky bastard. I crouched while raising myself as the roof of the cave would allow, touching the wall closest to me, searching for some way to climb back to the surface.

At this point the coffin was quite narrow and I was sure I was close to its center. Through the mist I thought I could see roots dangling from the lid, extending all the way to where I stood, but when I came closer, I could see they were bronze chains. Each was thick as my wrist and covered with the same slick fungus that made the tree roots impossible to climb.

This coffin was large, a lot like ones that ancient nobles had been buried in. The one Wang and I were trapped in would be the outer coffin or the coffin chamber. It contained the coffin that held the body, which was the inner coffin. This inner coffin was placed in the center of the outer one, with a dozen or so wood coffins encasing it as protection. Why did this coffin chamber have no trace of the inner coffin? Was there nothing in here but us? Then what had made those weird clicking noises or caused the electromagnetic transmissions that had interfered with my walkie-talkie?

Puzzled, I walked over to examine the chains, took one step, and plunged forward into emptiness. I grabbed one of the closest chains and stopped my body from sliding into what my flashlight showed me was a deep hole in the floor.

I had seen this before when I was in the undersea tomb; this hole in the center of the chamber was called a coffin well. Below it was where the inner coffin would be found. The bronze chains that hung around it were probably what had lowered the inner coffin into the well.

As I pieced this together, Wang flung himself out of the mist, brandishing something and shrieking wildly. As he rocketed toward me, I called, "Stop! Don't move another step!" But my warning came too late.

"Shit!" he shrieked as he plunged into the coffin well. The chains around me began to quiver and I knew he had probably grabbed them to stop his fall. Then my hands began to slip down the chain that I clutched and I too resumed my slide into the gaping hole of the well.

"That damned fungus!" I yelled. I'd clutched the chain too tightly. I'd squeezed the mushroomlike growths so hard that they exuded a creamy waxen liquid and coated the chain with an oily slickness. I jammed the blade of my hunting knife into a tree root that had grown along the length of the chain and stopped my descent.

I had slid at least thirty feet down and was inside the coffin well. Mr. Wang hung from a chain about a foot below me, his face covered with blood. He had removed his belt and tied one end to his arm and the other into a link of the chain. I had to give him credit for being resourceful.

As my flashlight beam struck him, he glared at me. "You're a dead man, you son of a bitch," he growled.

"There's nothing you can do to me now, old man," I said,

and he spat at me as I began to examine where we were.

The coffin well was within the trunk of the bronze tree, which was carved in the same design as the outer portion, bearing the shape of the double-bodied serpent. The mist in here was much less thick than in the coffin chamber and I could see that the well was rectangular, about twelve feet long and six feet wide, just the right size to hold a coffin. Its walls had only a sprinkling of the mushrooms clinging to the surface, which I noticed with relief. Perhaps I could climb out of this place after all.

I looked down and saw the bronze chains extending far beyond the rays of my flashlight. Where is the bottom of this well, I wondered, and where does the trunk of this tree end? Could the entire tree be hollow? What purpose was it created for?

There was a peculiar odor that seemed to be getting stronger by the second. It stung my nose like tear gas, and my eyes began to water. Then the clicking noise began again, somewhere close by.

"Listen," Wang hissed. "It's coming from below us in the well."

CHAPTER THIRTY-FOUR
RECONCILIATION

The sound echoed as though it were coming from the bottom of the well and the chains quivered with every click, as though responding to a heartbeat produced by a gigantic artery. What could move anything as heavy as those linked pieces of bronze?

Mr. Wang was surprisingly calm as he listened. Impassive, he lit a cigarette and took a long, relaxed puff. Then he took a little tube from his pocket, shook it twice as though it were a thermometer, and held it as it began to emit a fluorescent glow.

When it beamed brightly, he tossed it down into the well; it gave off a small streak of light as it dropped. I could hear it hit something with a small impact and then there was an explosive bang. Before the rod continued its descent and disappeared, I could see something suspended from the chains far below us. It looked like a coffin made of yellow crystal.

When Wang saw this, he untied the belt that anchored him to the chain and slid down into the darkness without a word. Reluctant to have him explore alone, I pulled my hunting knife from the root that had secured it and quickly followed.

Within a matter of seconds, Wang was at the bottom of the well. As soon as I saw him, I wrapped my legs around the chain to stop my descent and looked around.

There were no tree roots here, the walls were bare, and the fluorescent stick lay on the floor, still giving off its weird glow. Nearby was the bulk of a coffin, shrouded in darkness. I grabbed my flashlight from where I'd tucked it into my waistband and directed its rays to illuminate the mass of stone that rested before us.

It wasn't a coffin but a huge rock that was shaped like one, giving off the unmistakable gleam of amber. I gasped; a slab of amber this size would be priceless, if only it were possible to get it out in one piece. Suspended in the honeyed glow of this gigantic gem was a black shadow in the shape of a human, curled up in a fetal position, trapped within the amber like a fly.

Wang was less in awe than I; he walked toward the stone and kicked at it viciously.

"Stop that," I yelled. "Don't damage this; it's the most magnificent piece of amber I've ever seen."

"What are you talking about?" he sneered. "This is just a cocoon for corpses." He kicked at it again; the cocoon quivered a bit but remained undamaged.

I slid the rest of the way down and approached the block of amber, my hunting knife drawn and ready.

"Listen to me," Wang said as I drew closer. "We have to work together or we'll both die. This isn't a place either of us could get out of on our own."

He was right, I realized. Even so, I'd be a fool to trust this guy. Caution was essential so long as he was around.

"I need to tell you what happened with my walkie-talkie

earlier, when you were trying to reach me." I described the weird interference that had kept us from communicating. Wang looked dubious and turned on his own equipment. Harsh static tore into the stillness, a high-pitched buzzing that sounded like a long, rasping shriek. Wang quickly switched it off.

"Holy shit," he muttered. "I misjudged you. Sorry. But then you weren't so easy on me either—my jaw still aches from what you handed out. We're even—let's put this little feud of ours on hold until we get out of here, okay?"

I nodded, thinking yeah right, you plan to kill me when you no longer need me, and Lao Yang too. Good luck with that. And I know you're aware that I'll get rid of you and that slimeball Liang the second I can do that. We grinned at each other, both knowing the other wasn't to be trusted for a second.

"Let's get down to business," Wang said. "Look at that shape wrapped inside the cocoon. Does this thing look human to you?"

"I have no idea," I replied. "From what I've read about corpse cocoons, they're usually much smaller than this, about the size of washbasins. Some resemble jade while others look as though they were made of amber. The ones dug up in Sichuan and Inner Mongolia usually held children or small animals, rarely an adult. This shape looks large enough to be a full-grown person, but who knows? What do you think?"

"My grandfather told me that when he owned a Hong Kong pawn shop before the Japanese invasion, rich men came to sell him these things, hoping to finance their escape before it was too late. The cocoons all came in different sizes, and each held different objects. Some, my grandfather said, contained humans. Later when I had my own business, I saw cocoons like this but never so big. And never until now have I come across one that I couldn't look into without having to break it open. With this one, all I can see is liquid floating inside the amber, around that shape."

"This is hopeless, no matter what the cocoon contains or how valuable the amber may be," I said. "We certainly can't bring it back up with us; it's much too big and heavy."

Wang shrugged and for the first time he looked discouraged. "What did Mr. Lee mean when he told me that once we got here, we would get everything we wanted?"

"Maybe that wasn't what he meant. Maybe he didn't mean that the place contained everything you wanted, only that once you reached it, you could wish for whatever you wanted and your wish would come true. The old man who advised me before I started this journey had shown me a photo of a cave painting with people bowing to a bronze tree. An inscription under the painting said that they were preparing to offer blood sacrifices to ensure that the tree would grant their wishes. Maybe Mr. Lee simply meant that this tree was a place where dreams came true."

"You could be on the right track with this," Wang agreed. "When we fell into the coffin chamber, I was ahead of you and I ran to hide in the mist—but first I saw the bronze chains and quickly examined them. The ground near them was solid then but when I returned to attack you, there was a hole where none had been a few minutes before. I was too stunned by my fall to give this any thought but—this is the weird thing: when I ran over to look at the chains, I thought there really should be a coffin well near them and when I returned, there it was. Did my wish come true?"

Crazy old man, I thought, when I hit him, I must have addled his senile little brain.

"I can see you don't believe me," Wang continued, "but I'm telling you the absolute truth."

"Hmm," I replied. "Perhaps what Mr. Lee really meant was that once you come to this place, your subconscious mind will affect what is here and transform reality. If the bronze tree has that kind of power, then maybe we're imagining everything we see here. We wished for the coffin and the treasure within it and even corpses that would prove we had found the real thing—the tree could have conjured up all that in response to our wishes, couldn't it?"

Perhaps everything—including the Deadly Dragons and the monkeys and the killer salmon the size of a whale—were all created in response to our wish for adventure, I realized; then my mind ran away with me and I fell silent.

Oh shit, I thought, that bronze tree branch that Lao Yang and his cousin dug up, the one the cousin secretly came away with—it was part of this tree, I'm sure. Did the cousin know what power the tree possessed? And did it make him go mad? Lao Yang is the one who has the branch now—does he know the secret of this tree?

There was one way to test whether this was true or not. All I had to do was make a wish—or watch Mr. Wang make one. Somehow neither possibility made me feel very secure.

34. RECONCILIATION

Then a wave of fear hit me hard. I had no idea of who this man Wang was. He could be anyone—perhaps his name was something altogether different—how would I ever know?

CHAPTER THIRTY-FIVE

OUT OF CONTROL

I stared at the man beside me, who was so absorbed in thought that he didn't notice my gaze. When I had seen him in the campground, I had paid little attention to him and had no clear memory of that first sighting to compare with the person who now claimed to be Mr. Wang. Yet I had a strong intuition that this man was not who he said he was.

"Mr. Wang," I whispered, "don't move." Slowly I inched my way toward him.

"You look familiar to me now," I said. "I know who you really are." I watched his eyes dart like frightened goldfish in a small tank. "In fact I know you all too well. What the hell do you think you're doing, Lao Yang?"

Wang began to laugh hysterically; his fat body began to lose its bulk like a flattening bicycle tire. His face gradually relaxed and took on the familiar features of my old friend.

He stretched, yawned, and said, "Almost tricked you—you always thought I was such a dolt. Does this change your opinion?"

"What sort of bullshit is this anyway?"

"Listen to me for once and I'll tell you the whole story—but only if you shut up and let me do the talking."

If Lao Yang had the power to transform his appearance as

he just had, what else was he capable of? Why had he brought me to this place? It couldn't be a matter of money and treasure; his new powers could have gained him anything he wanted without going through the dangers this trip had beset upon us. What did he hope to gain by coming here?

One thing was certain—he'd set a trap for me and I fell right into it. He had lied to me and I swallowed everything he told me. So much for friendship. If I could only have his power for five minutes, I'd turn him into a pig, kill him, roast him, and eat every scrap of his flesh, I told myself.

Lao Yang watched me closely. He knew me well and was aware that beneath my silence was a killing rage. But not even his new abilities told him how to calm me down; I knew that from the puzzled look in his eyes.

Suddenly he sighed, took a photo out of his pocket, and said, "Look at this. Let me explain this whole thing to you, okay?"

He handed me the picture and trained the beam of his flashlight upon it so I could see it clearly. It was his mother, but I could barely recognize her. When I last saw her, she was young and beautiful. In this photo, she was grey and hunched and careworn. She looked nothing like the woman I used to call Pretty Aunt.

"What do you want to tell me? What does your mother have to do with all this?"

"I lied to you, you know. I didn't come here for money. I came for my mother. When I got out of prison, she was gone."

"You mean she died?"

He looked at the photo and nodded. "When I went home after I was released, I opened the door and smelled something horrible. My mother was slumped over her sewing machine, motionless. I ran to her, thinking she was asleep but when I tried to pick her up, I knew she was dead." He closed his eyes and grimaced to keep from crying as he spoke.

"After she was in her coffin, I sat in our empty house alone, not daring to sleep for fear that I would see my mother's dead face again. I sat without moving for nine days, hoping I would starve myself to death. But then I smelled a mouthwatering aroma from the kitchen as though someone was cooking. I got up to see what was going on and there was my mother, smiling at me and saying, 'Don't be impatient; it will be ready for you in a few minutes.' I thought I was hallucinating from grief and exhaustion, but she didn't go away. I swear, the guy who came to deliver vegetables saw her. She had really come back, looking the same as she had before I went to prison—even the food she made for me was exactly what I had eaten when I was growing up.

"She wasn't a ghost," he continued, "but I knew there was something very wrong. One night I was watching TV and the electricity went off in my neighborhood—every house went dark, except for mine. My TV stayed on all night long, even after I unplugged it. Soon after that my cousin wrote to me saying weird things were happening to him too in prison; his life was going just the way he wanted it, no hitches, no problems, all perfect. It had to be connected with that bronze branch that he stole, he told me.

"I began to do some research and learned that the branch must have come from the Wishing Tree of the Serpent God that appeared in so many ancient histories. The good things that were happening to me and to my cousin were granted to us by this tree and I was sure that we could use it to our advantage. But when I tried to control this power, things went terribly wrong. One morning I woke up and saw my mother with her back turned toward me, sitting at her sewing machine. When I called to her, she didn't seem to hear me. I walked over to her and I saw her face..."

Lao Yang stopped, choking with sobs. He gasped for breath, waving his hands helplessly. I tried not to imagine what he had seen.

He grabbed a cigarette from the empty air and it lit without striking a match. He took a long drag and went on. "I know how dangerous this power is. But I want my mother to come back to life. I needed to find someone to come with me, someone who once knew her and who had never been touched by the power of this damned tree. So I chose you."

"But, Lao Yang, it sounds like this is against all rules of nature. The dead can't come back to life."

"All I'm asking is to get back the three years I lost with my mother when I was in prison, and to be with her when she dies a peaceful death. That's all. You knew my mother; she was always good to you. You wouldn't want her to die alone the way she did and rot unattended, would you?"

I shook my head, rocked with a wave of real anguish. If Lao Yang's mother returned from the grave, I would never dare to visit his house again. Nobody knew who had put this bronze tree here or what his intentions were but they didn't seem to have been anything but evil. How could his mother ever be loving and good if she were brought back to life by this sort of horrible power?

"I can't do this, Lao Yang. Your mom is dead. She's already returned to dust. You should...you should just let her go. Don't drag her out of her grave, please."

Lao Yang smiled. "It's too late, you don't understand.

Whether you want to help me or not is irrelevant. It's why I couldn't tell you about this until now. I've achieved my goal with you."

"What do you mean?"

"Try it for yourself. Make something appear."

I looked at my hand and imagined a stone within it; I wished for it to appear. Nothing happened.

"You see? When you want to use it, the power won't come." Lao Yang laughed. "It only arrives under specific conditions. You can guide it but you can't be its master. Even if you were starving, it wouldn't send you a roast duck like a food delivery service."

"You mean a person's mind is a passive vessel for this power to use as it wishes?"

He nodded. "That's right. Take what I said to you just now as an example. It could already have guided your thoughts to travel hundreds of miles to my house and put my mother back in it."

"You," I said through lips stiff with fear, "are completely out of your fucking mind."

Before Lao Yang could reply, the bronze tree and the amber corpse cocoon shook violently. We almost fell as the ground beneath us quaked and we grabbed the nearest chains to keep us steady. Looking into the darkness below, we could see something crawling up in our direction. Every time it moved, the tree vibrated and the earth began to shake harder than ever. We swayed as we clung to the chains.

"Tell me," I asked Lao Yang, "those clicking sounds? Did you make them?"

"Yes, of course. I needed to lure you down into the coffin chamber. And I caused the static and interference so you wouldn't hear me fighting with the real Mr. Wang when I knocked him out and stole his identity.

"So is this crawling creature your creation too?"

"No and it's scaring the shit out of me. Tell me. What was your first impression of this bronze tree?"

I shuddered. "I thought it grew straight out of hell. You don't think the devil is climbing up toward us, do you?"

"Don't talk that way, you moron," Lao Yang kicked at me as he shouted, then he stopped as he muttered, "Oh no, oh shit—look."

Out of the darkness below emerged a gigantic eyeball, its purple pupil one long thin vertical line, like the eye of a cat.

CHAPTER THIRTY-SIX

LANDSLIDE

As the huge eye came closer, the bronze tree shook even more violently—and so did I. Lao Yang's complexion was so white with fear that he almost glowed in the dark. "How in the hell did your brain conjure this thing up?"

"I've never seen or dreamed of anything like this before. It isn't anything the damned power of the tree has plucked from my subconscious," I yelled back at him.

"The hell with it," he blustered. "It's only an eyeball—it's not like it can bludgeon us to death with its lashes. When it gets close enough, I'll kick it straight into blindness."

His words barely hit the air when a huge tentacle rose up from the dark, striking the amber cocoon. It shattered and the corpse inside broke into four pieces and hurtled down into the abyss.

The impact of this blow had Lao Yang and me spinning on our chains, which we clung to for dear life.

"Damn you," I shouted at Lao Yang. "You have the power to materialize stupid things like cigarettes—make a cannon appear instead and blow whatever this thing is into smithereens."

Lao Yang cursed, "Damn you, you have no idea of what you're talking about. You think it's that simple? We need to haul ass and get out of this place now."

Without another word, we began to scale the bronze chains but our hands soon slipped. Neither of us had the strength to move further. I thought of the fungus that waited for us on the tree roots above and I knew we were dead men.

And then Lao Yang lifted his arms, climbing as agilely as a monkey, as he pulled me along behind him.

"Can't you just make a ladder appear?" I grumbled.

"Can't you just fuck off," he grumbled as he inched his way along the chains. He gave a huge tug and pulled me with him back into the coffin chamber.

The mist had disappeared and I wanted to examine the bas-relief that had been hidden earlier.

"Bad idea," Lao Yang warned. "We have to keep climbing—we're not safe yet."

Again the gigantic tentacle lashed up from the well and sent the massive stone coffin lid flying up like a windblown paper bag. The force of the blow broke the surrounding tree roots into wood chips and the bronze tree swayed as though rocked by a hurricane.

The air was a swirl of wood fragments, bark, and dust. Large chips hurtled past like stray bullets, hitting and destroying the nearby boardwalk. It was as though a bomb had been detonated and Lao Yang and I found ourselves stunned, lying outside the coffin.

The tentacle seemed to have lost its strength now that it had ventured out of its hiding place; it flailed about blindly and it was easy for us to avoid its reach. Lao Yang pointed down to the area where the boardwalk remained undamaged. "If we don't get down there now, who knows what will come out of that damned well to kill us."

"But we can't abandon Mr. Wang," I protested and turned to look for him. He was nowhere to be seen.

"Forget about him," Lao Yang yelled. "We have to save ourselves." He grabbed the rope that Wang and I had used to reach this place and we both clung to it, just as the lid of the coffin plunged back to earth, crashing onto the platform and breaking it to bits.

"Swing over to safety now!" I yelled, but my words were punctuated by a loud explosion. The coffin chamber bulged and cracked, and a huge black serpent emerged. It had only one eye, and I shuddered as I recognized it as the cat's eye that had stared at us from the coffin well. The scales on its body were very small; it looked quite a bit like a mammoth insect.

"Shit," Lao Yang shouted, "the tentacle is that thing's tail!" He hurtled forward with all of his strength and our rope arced into empty air, placing us safely on the boardwalk below.

The second we landed, Lao Yang grabbed his rifle from where it was secured to his backpack, aimed at the serpent's eye, and fired. The bullet struck and the serpent shrieked, rolling into a ball. Its tail swept toward us, smashing a section of the boardwalk above the spot where we were standing.

Lao Yang continued to shoot; I knew his gun held no more than five rounds of ammunition but it fired nonstop with no need to reload. Odd how this power comes across for us sometimes and leaves us in the lurch at other points when we could use it, I thought.

But the caliber of the rifle lacked the power to pierce the

reptile's armor of scales. It had rolled into a ball to protect its eye, which seemed to be its only vulnerable point. All that Lao Yang's firepower did was to keep the monster motionless—except for its damned tail.

"This is no use—run!" I shouted. We raced to the gaping chasm in the boardwalk and I began to scale the cliff. "What the hell are you doing?" Lao Yang sputtered. Grabbing me, he leaped onto the boardwalk below. It buckled under our weight and gave way, and we landed on the ground at the very bottom of the boardwalk, with the serpent slithering its way down the bronze tree trunk, coming to get us.

Below us were many small caves, much too tiny for the serpent to crawl into. We hastily crawled down and squirmed into the smallest one we could find. We barely made it inside when the eye of the serpent, bloody and terrible, filled the cavern's entrance. Lao Yang shot at it but this time his bullets had no effect.

The serpent's head was easily the size of one of Chairman Mao's Liberation tanks, much too huge to squeeze through the opening. In a rage, the monster withdrew and began to butt and flail at the cliff that held our cave. We could hear the pounding of rocks, loosened and falling around our sanctuary. A crack appeared in the cavern roof above us and Lao Yang pulled me deeper into the recesses of our small hiding place.

There was a crashing sound as rocks and gravel pelted us and the cave filled with a cloud of dust. I curled into a ball, covering my head as boulders dropped from above like deadly raindrops. Then with a boom, a rock the size of a truck fell in front of the cave's entrance, sealing us inside.

The serpent became even more frenzied in its efforts to tear the cliff to pieces; the noise of its destruction was deafening.

"He's not giving up," Lao Yang muttered. "A few more minutes of this and we're done for. We have to find a way out before this cliff collapses."

Our backs were against the end of the cavern wall. There was nowhere else to go. "Think of a god to pray to, my friend," I replied. "Even if we had dynamite with us, we couldn't use it in this small space without blowing ourselves sky-high."

The serpent roared above us. We could feel the impact of his blows and the noise of a wall of rock toppling. And there, behind us, appeared the entrance to a larger, deeper cave.

"Let's go!" I shouted but Lao Yang leaped in front of me.

"We can't go into that place. Keep away from it!"

CHAPTER THIRTY-SEVEN

THE DIARY

"Are you out of your mind? This new cave is the only hope we have of saving ourselves. Would you rather be buried alive?" I screamed, as rocks thundered around us.

"You have no idea what's waiting for us in there. Think this through."

"Shit, we don't have time to think, asshole. No matter what we find in there, whether it's a dragon's pool or a tiger's den, it's better than what's going on out here." I stepped toward the entrance but Lao Yang grabbed my arm.

"Just listen to me for once, damn you. You really can't go into this cave!"

Then a rock fell; I gave a huge tug, breaking Lao Yang's hold on me just as the boulder landed in front of us, blocking the entrance to the newly emerged cave and sending us to the ground once again.

The minute I could think again, I realized we were trapped.

I pushed against the fallen rock but it was immovable. I climbed up on the surrounding debris and saw that this had probably been one large cave once but had been separated into two chambers by an earlier collapse long ago. As I explored, I could hear the serpent's attack waning. Its crashes became less and less thunderous and then ceased altogether.

As my mind cleared, I remembered how Lao Yang had clutched my arm as the rock plunged toward us. If I hadn't pulled away, we'd both be meat pancakes by now. I glared at him, yelling, "What the hell is wrong with you? You could have killed us just now."

Blocked from coming near by the rock that lay between us, Lao Yang shouted back, "What are you talking about? You were the one who put us in danger, trying to get in that cave. Now what?"

I scrabbled away at the debris and could see the beam of Lao Yang's flashlight, but the boulder that separated us was the size of a small house. There was a space between it and the wall that only my arm could fit through, not my body.

I picked up a sizable rock and began to hammer it against the boulder. Tiny crumbles of stone broke away from the obstacle but no cracks appeared.

"Stop!" Lao Yang bellowed. "The vibrations from your pounding are loosening rocks from the cavern roof. The whole thing will come down around our ears!"

"We're finished either way—would you rather be crushed to death or starve to death? What difference does it make?"

"Stop, I said! Use your head, not your arms. Take another look around and tell me if you see anything interesting."

I looked around. It was pitch-dark and all I could see were rocks.

37. THE DIARY

"There's nothing here," I said.

"Really? There's nothing? Look carefully."

"Why would I lie? This place where I'm standing is as small as your dick. If there were anything to see, I'd notice it."

Lao Yang said, "Well, take a second look and I'll investigate here. Maybe there's a crevice I can slip through to get over to your side of the cave."

Then the rays of his flashlight moved away. I leaned against the boulder. There's no way out of here, I told myself. I stared at the rock that had us trapped. The damned thing had to weigh several tons. I was moving away when I saw something—there was a drawing of some kind on the far side of the boulder.

At first sight, I thought it was some kind of primitive cave painting done by the workers who had cast the bronze tree but when I looked closer, I knew I was wrong. It was a drawing of an airplane, embellished with words in English.

Who could have done this?

The drawing was partially covered with small rocks and gravel; I dug to clear them away and tried to figure out what in hell the drawing meant. I removed a big chunk of rock and black fabric emerged, looking like a piece of ragged clothing.

I tugged at it and out of nowhere popped a skeletal human hand, all bones. It was contorted into a claw as if it had tried to dig its way out of the pile of rubble that covered it.

How did a dead man end up in this place? Had he been

buried alive when the cave collapsed back in the past? Who could he have been?

I continued to move the rocks away until I found the body, which looked as if it had been here for quite some time. An amulet hung around its neck. Could this body have belonged to a grave robber? Was it somehow related to the corpse I had seen at the bottom of the waterfall? Was I soon to join the two of them?

I dug until the entire body was exhumed and uncovered a small backpack nearby. It was almost threadbare. I looked inside and saw something black. When I turned the pack upside down, a notebook fell out.

It was almost destroyed by mildew, but the paper was of the highest quality so the pages were still intact and words written in blue ink were still legible. The front pages were an address book and of no interest but when I flipped past the names and phone numbers, I was stunned. There were diary entries, dated from three years back, scrawled in an unformed, childish script, with only a hundred words or so in each entry.

I skimmed through the pages, feeling sick as I read. The diary began when this person was trapped in the cave. "Out of eighteen men who came here," the first entry said, "I am the only one left."

He and his group had found this place after traveling through a huge banyan forest, probably the same one Lao Yang had found with his cousin. It had been a dangerous route; only six of the original eighteen were still alive after traveling along that path. The rest got here by climbing down a tunnel in a hollow banyan tree.

They also had discovered the boardwalk and the burial

platform; beyond that was only a deep, green pool that seemed bottomless, or so they found after diving into it. When they got out of the water, they found that the level of the pool had dropped drastically and continued to lose ground as they watched.

Some of the group decided to explore the bronze tree by climbing it while the rest of them crawled into one of the caves that dotted the side of the cliff. The writer of the diary was one who entered the cave.

Soon after he came inside, he heard a strange sound and looked out to see a large black serpent, as huge as a dragon, coil out of the pool. It writhed its way up the trunk of the bronze tree; then he heard shrieks from his comrades, the sounds of gunfire, and then silence.

An explosion rocked the cave and he knew that before dying, one of the men had detonated an explosive that he carried with him. It had the force of a bomb; its blast collapsed the cave that the writer and his group were in.

When the writer of the diary regained consciousness, he was alone, trapped in the cave. For seven days he lived on the small amount of food and water that he had in his backpack. Then his flashlight batteries died and he knew he soon would too.

Within a few days he began to hallucinate from thirst, picked up his empty water bottle, and without thinking raised it to his lips.

Sweet, fresh water flowed from the empty jug and he drank for a long time without stopping. It was impossible for him to drain it dry; the water kept flowing no matter how much he drank.

I've gone insane, he thought, but if I'm hallucinating,

maybe I can dream up some food. Reaching into his provision sack that he had emptied days before, he found it was crammed to the brim with food. He ate until he was ready to vomit.

This is real, he thought, as he fought against waves of nausea, it's insane but it's really happening. Whatever appeared before him was somehow connected to his own thoughts, but not in a specific way. If he wanted roast pork, he didn't get it but when he was hungry, some sort of food would appear in endless quantities.

He began to analyze this power and experiment with it, trying to turn his thoughts into material objects, which he wrote about in detail. In the end his only conclusion was he had accidentally turned into some sort of god.

Before he died he used his pen to draw on the rock. In his final writing he said he would try to use his power to free himself—if he succeeded he would know he was a relative of Superman. If he failed he would let himself die.

I looked at this man's body and felt overwhelmingly pessimistic. If his power didn't gain him his freedom, what good was it? And what did that tell me about my eventual fate? I probably wouldn't even last a week.

I rummaged through the pockets of the corpse's shredded jacket. There was a cell phone with a dead battery, a wallet with a little cash, and the dead man's ID card. I could see a badly blurred photo and words below that looked as though they might be legible. I struggled to puzzle out what looked as though it might be the dead man's name.

37. THE DIARY

CHAPTER THIRTY-EIGHT

STRANGER IN THE DARKNESS

"What are you looking at?" Lao Yang's voice came from behind me.

I grunted a reply, still enmeshed in my thoughts. The man who wrote this diary had been here three years ago; so had Lao Yang. Had Lao Yang come here with more people than just his cousin? I dismissed that idea immediately; what this man wrote about was completely different from Lao Yang's story.

I looked at the faded name on the ID card and then I shuddered. I knew this name almost as well as my own. Jie Ziyang was Lao Yang's real name.

"What did you find?" he called again.

I had to squeeze out my reply. "Don't bother me. I just found something very interesting and I need to examine it."

"Show me," he said, his eyes peering through the darkness at my hands.

I couldn't reply. Beneath that familiar name was a birth date. It was the same as Lao Yang's.

Am I looking at the body of my oldest friend? I asked myself. But if so, who is this person who came to me, stammering and subservient, fresh out of prison, to persuade me to come with him to this place? Whose pallid face is watching me from the other side of this boulder?

I instinctively stepped farther back, doing my best to get away from the rock that divided me from whoever stood behind it. I could see a motionless shadow peering in my direction as I tried to shrink silently into the darkness.

This man knew I had found him out. If he still clung to the identity of my comrade, he'd be yelling curses at me by now. Instead he made no sound at all.

My frozen brain struggled to make sense of all this. Who had taken on Lao Yang's identity so completely that I had been fooled for weeks? True, there were parts of his personality that were far more adventurous and resourceful than the man I had grown up with, but I chalked that up to what he had learned during his years in prison. It had never occurred to me that someone might be impersonating him.

A voice came out of the darkness. "I tried to keep you from entering that cave but you wouldn't listen. Not all knowledge is good; some things should never come to light. Your obstinacy has brought us to this point."

"You aren't Lao Yang. Who in hell are you?"

The voice laughed. "Who am I? I'm Lao Yang, Jie Ziyang, the guy who grew up with you and who was imprisoned for three years. If you don't believe me, go check my criminal record!"

"Bullshit. Lao Yang's body is right here next to me. He's been dead for three years, he wasn't in a jail cell. Tell me who you are."

The face that looked so much like my old friend peered through the crevice between the boulder and the cavern wall.

"You're right. He's been dead for three years but I'm still

alive. You had no idea that I wasn't your old pal; we've been getting along just fine up till now. So what does any of this matter? I'm Lao Yang now—get used to it."

"You're not my friend. You're not even human. You're the power of the tree in the shape of a man."

"You're going mad, you know. If you want to live, forget what's happened here and we'll carry on as we did before." The voice had turned so cold that my entire body shook as I heard it.

A rifle barrel protruded through the crevice and I leaped farther back into darkness. I could feel the force of the bullet whisk past my neck; a second shot broke off a large chunk of the boulder that shielded me from whatever was on the opposite side.

I hurled a large rock at the rifle barrel and knocked it aside. My second missile was even heavier and struck the barrel, bending it so it was useless. I heard a few curses from the other side of the rock; then all was blackness and silence once more.

"It's dark now," the voice said. "You've always been afraid of the dark, haven't you? Be careful of what you imagine. It will probably come true, and if you turn on your flashlight, there it will be, right beside you."

The bastard was right; I was afraid of the dark and always had been.

I struggled to keep my mind clear of any menacing thoughts but my fear got the upper hand. I could feel a presence inches away from my face; its breath was hot on my skin and the air was filled with a foul odor as though something was rotting nearby.

It's all my imagination, I told myself, nothing could take

shape so quickly, before I even visualized my fears. There's nothing near me, no danger at hand. This creature is trying to use my fear as a weapon against me; don't allow him to do that.

I took a deep breath, then felt an ice-cold dampness sweep past me, turning my body numb. He's right; there is something in this space with me, I thought. I pressed my back against the wall but behind me there was no stone, only hundreds of small scales, cold and horribly slimy and wriggling under my shoulders.

I grabbed my flashlight as I heard the voice taunt, "Go on—turn on that light. You're not afraid to see what is behind you, are you now? Come on—I'll help you figure out what's there. What else are friends for?"

A flashlight flooded through the crevice and its rays revealed a gigantic python, its hood inches from my nose and its coils wrapped around my feet, filling the space where I stood. Frightened by the light, the snake writhed and its scales whispered a threatening hiss that filled my head with its menace.

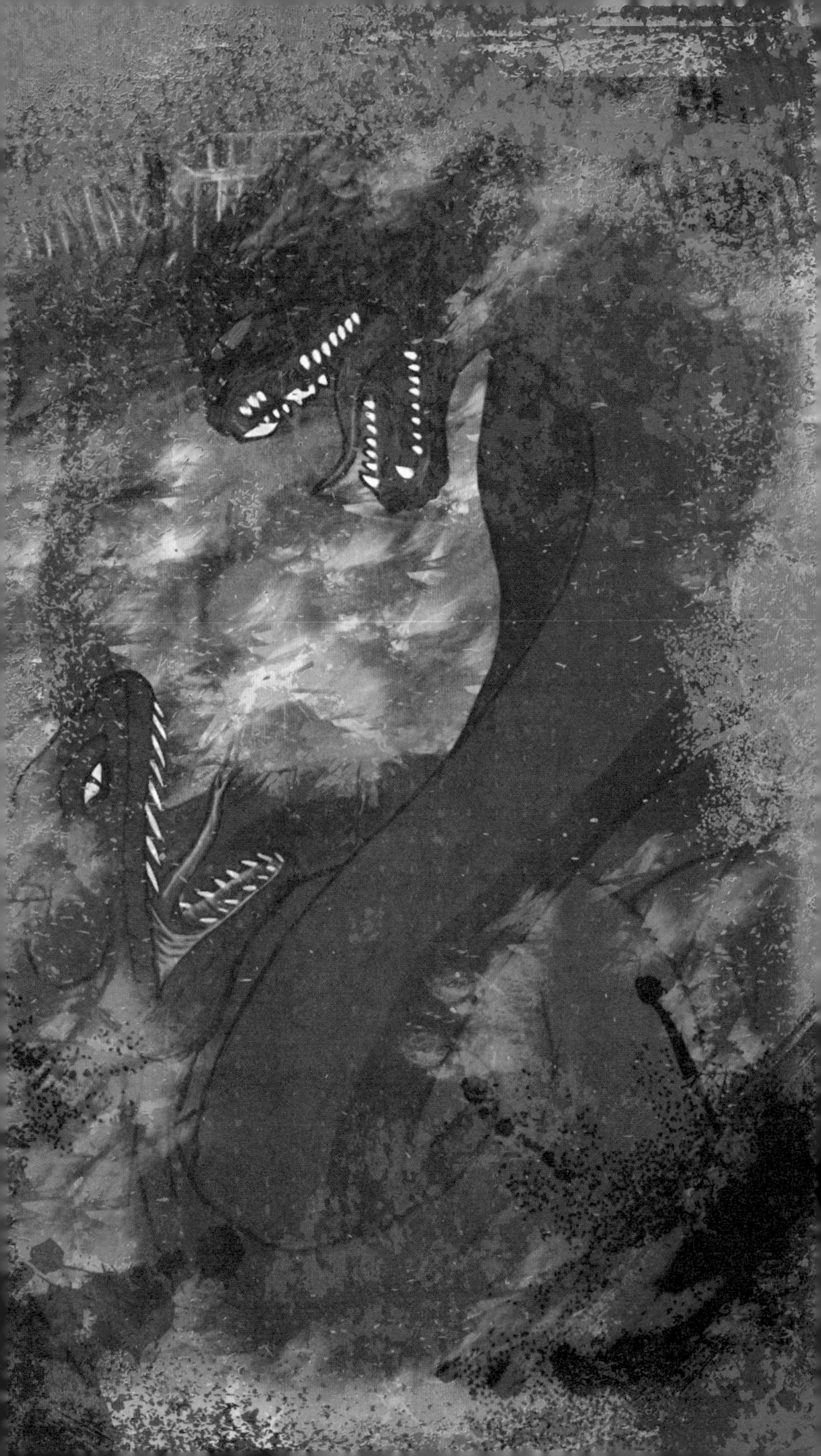

CHAPTER THIRTY-NINE

CANDLELIGHT

As the python stretched its huge tongue toward my face, I could see nothing else. I fought against the hysterical panic that threatened my sanity; how could this serpent be so real when it was only a piece of my own fear? And yet I knew it could kill me in a heartbeat if I didn't stay calm.

I knew pythons had incredible senses of sight and smell—and I'd read that they usually didn't hunt prey that was too small to provide them with a decent meal. I sat quietly, trying to shrink into a little ball of insignificance on the floor. Perhaps it would become disgusted and leave in search of something larger, like the man on the opposite side of the boulder.

I felt the serpent's tongue swipe at my ear, leaving a wet smear of saliva. Then it raised its head, stared at me for a second, and turned toward the light that came from behind the boulder. The crevice between the rock and the cavern wall was just about the size of the python's head. It pushed its hood against the opening, slithering toward the flashlight on the other side.

I could hear a string of frantic curses, and the flashlight clicked off. The python, blocked from reaching its goal because of its bulk, hurtled itself against the side of the boulder with the strength of an armored tank. The cave around me shook with a dreadful roar and the boulder flew off into the darkness like a child's paper kite. There was a horrible shriek. The sound of falling rocks echoed around the place where the man who claimed to be Lao Yang had been standing.

The python uncoiled itself in its new space, its hood reaching almost to the cavern's roof. It undulated in a horrible dance, curving and winding and hissing toward the body that lay before it. Trapped under fallen rock, there was the man who had tried to kill me, blood issuing from his open mouth instead of speech.

The python slithered past him to the cave's entrance and vanished into the night. I rushed to the man who stared at me with the same fear that I had felt myself just seconds before. His pelvis and legs were crushed under fallen stone and I was unable to free him.

"I can't help you," I whispered.

He looked at me, grimaced, and tossed his backpack over to me, then closed his eyes and lay still.

"Will I ever know who you are and what you meant to do with me?" I asked. An explosion of noise was the only reply as the entire cave quivered like jelly. I could hear the crack of rocks being dislodged above my head and I crawled rapidly toward the cavern's entrance.

I heard a croaking voice say, "Stop!" and as I turned I saw the crushed body behind me disappear under an avalanche of boulders. Hurtling out of the cave, I saw the lunge of a black shadow, striking the mountain wall behind me.

I turned and saw the one-eyed serpent from the coffin

well and the python locked together in a deadly embrace, two whirling cyclones of scales. Their tails whipped about, turning rocks into flying missiles and piles of powder.

A wild flail struck the spot where I was standing and sent me flying off the cliff into midair. I screamed as I struck something that gave way under my body and I descended into a cold, green silence. I was underwater, plunging down twenty feet beneath its surface.

Damn it. Where did this water come from? Where am I? I wondered as I sank.

I was sure I was hallucinating; I could feel arms grab me and lift me to the surface. When my vision cleared, I could see Liang swimming beside me.

He towed me out of the water, which turned out to be a huge pool. Its level rose higher and higher as we made our way out of it. Is this the pool that Lao Yang wrote about in his diary? I asked myself.

Liang had used all of his strength to rescue me and could move no further. I pulled him up to the trunk of the bronze tree and we both leaned against it in silence.

There was a roar, then a crash, and water showered about us. "Damn it, we're dead now!" I yelled. The python had rocketed into the pool, and crawling down the bronze tree in pursuit was the serpent from the coffin well.

Liang looked up, saw the huge purple cat's eye coming toward us, and shrieked, "Oh hell, where did this come from? This…this is a Zhu Jiuyin!"

I pulled him with me behind the bronze tree as I gasped, "What do you mean?"

"Zhu Jiuyin was called the Candle Dragon long ago, but really it's a gigantic poisonous snake dating back to prehistoric times. When mankind began to use oil from its body to make candles, it became extinct. How could there be one here and now?"

"Don't look at its eye," Liang continued. "Legends say that if it gives you a look, it will turn you into a monster with the head of a man and the body of a snake."

We were lucky. The Zhu Jiuyin wasn't interested in us. Its attention was entirely claimed by the giant python. It stared into the pool, looking for its adversary, who was still hidden in the water's depths.

The water level kept rising and the pool advanced closer and closer to us. If it got high enough, I hoped, we'd be able to climb out of this place—if we didn't drown first or were eaten by the two battling reptiles. If only we could float to the top, we might have a chance of survival.

"I have a plan," I whispered to Liang but he was staring at the pool, looking even more frightened than usual. Following his gaze, I saw familiar objects floating in the water—the masks that had contained the Deadly Dragons. As they turned and bobbed about on the water, it was obvious that the insects were not clinging to them.

"Shit," I yelled, "this is why the python hasn't emerged from the depths of the pool—the bugs are eating him alive." I switched on my flashlight and leaped into the water. There was the python, so covered by ravenous insects that its black scales were invisible. It was on its back with the Deadly Dragons clinging to its soft and vulnerable belly; no matter how it thrashed about, the snake was unable to dislodge the mouths that were busily devouring it.

The beams of my flashlight immediately distracted the

insects from their meal and they swarmed toward me like a school of sharks. Their approach was so swift that they surrounded me before I had time to react. There was only one thing to do—I bit my own hand as hard as I could, sinking my teeth deep into my flesh. Blood filled my mouth and I spat it into the water. The pool turned scarlet as I submerged my wounded hand.

The Deadly Dragons fled from the bloodstained water, forming a wall between me and the python. I swam back to Liang, who had scrambled up the bronze tree trunk in terror. He had drawn the attention of the Zhu Jiuyin, whose purple eye was now crimson with its lust for blood. Since the python was no longer available, it began slithering toward Liang, its tail lashing wildly.

CHAPTER FORTY

ESCAPE

The serpent's bloodshot eye caught mine and stared at me unblinking; I felt dizzy and sick, as though it were sucking my soul out of my eye sockets. I pulled my gaze away and looked at Liang. He was also caught by the same stare and looked straight at it, motionless. "Liang, look at me," I shouted, but he didn't even twitch in my direction.

The legend of the Zhu Jiuyin's gaze might be true, I realized, and Liang would be doomed if I couldn't break his hypnotic state. Rushing to the edge of the pool, I scooped up a handful of water and tossed it in Liang's direction. It missed him and hit the serpent instead.

Taken by surprise, the Zhu Jiuyin closed its eye, retracted its head, and launched its attack. I leaned backward, pushing myself flat against the bronze tree, and the serpent's head missed its mark. Near me was the backpack tossed to me by the man who had taken on the shape of Lao Yang. I grabbed it and reached inside. With any luck at all I'd find some dynamite.

The pack was stuffed full of food but I found nothing else. I almost threw the damned thing into the pool in my disappointment. The serpent was coiling for his second attack and I had no way to defend myself. I threw myself into the pool, still clutching the useless backpack. As I hit the water, the jaws of the Zhu Jiuyin closed around my legs and I knew it was ready for its kill.

My hand went into the backpack and this time I could feel the shape of a flare gun. I pulled the trigger and a roaring sound whistled through the pack. A wave of heat seared my hand that held the gun and I heard the serpent thrashing about in the water like the propeller of a jumbo jet.

Its mouth opened and dropped me into the pool. I swam to the safety of the shore before looking back. The signal flare had apparently fired into the serpent's mouth and now burned white-hot within its body. The smell of boiling oil filled the air, and clouds of blue smoke surrounded the body of the burning reptile.

Of course the oil in this creature was highly flammable or people in ancient times would never have used it to make candles. But who would ever have guessed that one signal flare inside its body could cause such a conflagration? I felt sick when I thought of how random my luck had been just now and what would have become of me had I not blundered into the discovery of the flare gun.

In its agony, the Zhu Jiuyin contorted its body, its tail beating wildly on the side of the mountain. A crack appeared under its flail, and then more and more—the mountainside was being segmented like an orange as the cracks grew wider, extending to the edge of the pool. Water gushed toward the crevices made by the death throes of the Zhu Jiuyin, then rushed through the cracks in a massive torrent.

I looked for Liang but there was no trace of him. Giving myself over to the rush of water, I let the current sweep me through the largest crevice, spinning and whirling as the flood carried me along what appeared to be a tunnel within the heart of the mountain. Then the flow lost its force and became a slow stream; I forced myself up to the surface and found I had been carried back to the underground river we had discovered only a few days before.

The river current was without turbulence and the water was warm; I floated along in a leisurely fashion, staring at the cavern walls on either side of me. Then something familiar caught my eye—bas-relief carvings on the rock that were augmented with paintings.

I floated peacefully along the river, staring at images of human sacrifice, bodies hanging on the bronze tree, streams of blood flowing down the trunk, corpses thrown into the interior of the hollow tree. It was quite a party.

Then came images of people pouring buckets of liquid into the hollow core of the tree; our old friend the Zhu Jiuyin made a guest appearance, surrounded by soldiers all bearing bows and spears. I could well understand why he was greeted in that fashion, but according to what I had once read he was worshipped as a sacred deity. Why was he now prey to be hunted down and slaughtered?

Everyone who took part in the ceremony was masked, except for one who appeared to be the leader. His clothing looked like that on the statue that I had seen earlier in the gorge; was the sculpture a likeness of him? I stared at his figure in the paintings; in every one of them, a serpent's head was attached to his neck. It didn't look like a mask. Had the leader been transformed by the gaze of the Zhu Jiuyin?

One thing seemed clear to me. I was certain that in addition to being worshipped, the bronze tree was part of a hunting ceremony and the bodies that had been hung on it may well have been bait to lure the Zhu Jiuyin from the bottomless abyss of the hollow bronze tree. But why did people go to such lengths to kill this beast?

The reliefs bore no answer. The last scene was of a celebration, with no clue about what was done with the slain Zhu Jiuyin. I sighed and gave up my questions; there were too many unanswered aspects of what I had just gone through. My flashlight battery had died and I could only float passively on the dark river.

My usual unease that came when I was without light began to engulf me. Was the level of the river going to raise me to safety or would I be carried to the depths where the Zhu Jiuyin had lived? Would I finally learn how far down the bronze tree extended? Would that be the spot where the tomb we had been seeking was placed?

Then light appeared ahead of me and a loud rumble of water filled my ears. Light! It had to be from the outside world. I tossed away my useless flashlight and began to swim toward it.

A flash of light blinded me, white and piercing. My body plunged forward and soared into nothingness.

Shit, I thought, another damned waterfall. I extended both arms in front of me, hoping to turn my fall into a controlled dive, and I prayed that I would land in deep water. My hands struck the unyielding surface of rocks, my head followed, and that was all I knew.

CHAPTER FORTY-ONE

THE LETTER

I was unconscious for three days. When I awoke, I was in a hospital bed with no idea of how I got there. All I could remember was spinning through a spume of water and the pain and blackness as my head hit the rocks. I tried to talk but all that came from my mouth were weird squawking sounds.

"Be still," a nurse told me. "This is normal. You suffered a severe concussion but there's no brain damage. You're going to be fine."

On the next day, the noises I made were comprehensible words and I asked a doctor, "Where am I? How did I get here?"

"You're in the Red Cross Hospital in the Beilin District of Xian; you were brought here on a stretcher by several policemen. I don't know where they found you, but since you have at least twenty broken bones, I know you must have fallen from a great height. You're lucky to be alive."

I could see that my upper torso and my left arm were encased in plaster, making me completely immobile. "When can I leave the hospital?" I asked, trying not to panic.

The doctor smiled. "Don't be in such a rush to go. You

won't even be able to leave your bed for two more weeks."

When one of the policemen who had rescued me heard that I could finally speak, he came to see me, bearing a basket of fruit. "Where did you find me?" I asked him.

"I didn't," he replied. "Some villagers from the hamlet of Nan Tian came across you on the banks of a river and carried you down to our station on a bamboo raft. They had tended to your injuries, which the doctor said was the reason you survived. They were the heroes who rescued you, not us."

That was odd, I thought, the last thing I remembered was hitting the water. How did I get to dry ground? And Nan Tian was at least seventy or eighty miles away from the spot where we began to climb the mountain. Had we traveled that far when we were underground?

I made up a story about getting lost while mountain climbing and expressed my utmost gratitude to the policeman. Then I called my shop assistant, Wang Meng, asking him to fly to Xian with money and clothing. He arrived the next day, paid my hospital bill, and bought me a cell phone and a laptop that would connect me with the world again. He assured me that business was the same as usual. "But nobody has heard from your Uncle Three," he added.

"So nothing has changed," I sighed and told him to return to the shop.

During my days in bed, I found myself thinking of Lao Yang. His diary was still buttoned in the pocket of my tattered shirt but it was so waterlogged that it was completely illegible. Bored and frustrated, I switched on my laptop and went on the Internet.

There was no information about the bronze tree, and inquiries that I sent to friends bore no fruit either, except for one reply from America. "There was a discovery similar to the one you describe. It was a section of a bronze tree called the Column, found in a mine in the city of Panzihua in 1984. It was documented in ancient classical texts as being used to capture the underground serpent, the Zhu Jiuyin. Using fresh blood as a lure, they tricked it to come from the safety of the bronze tree and then killed it to make candles."

"Interesting indeed," I wrote back, "but is there any documentation stating the Column carried supernatural powers?'

He replied with a portion of an ancient novel that described an event that had taken place during the Qing dynasty. The emperor Qianlong was given a box made of pale jade, carved with the design of a dragon; when he opened it, he sent everyone away and that night called for some of his ministers to join him. They talked until midnight; later that night a fire broke out in the palace, killing all of the ministers who had been at that meeting except for one. The emperor never revealed what he had seen in the box or what he had discussed with his ministers, but the rumor was that the box contained the secret of the bronze tree and its powers.

"If you ever find this tree," he concluded, "you need to bring it to light so its secrets can be known to the world." I read this and smiled. Not me, I thought, I'm done with that damned thing.

A month later, I went home at last, began to pull myself together, and resumed my normal life. As I cleaned out my overstuffed mailbox, under the mountain of magazines and newspapers I found a letter.

My Old Comrade:

I didn't die. Or you could say I began another life.

I apologize for dragging you into this mess but after all, you're the only person I ever trusted. I had no other choice.

Now that this has come to an end, our friendship is over too. We've been close for so long but that doesn't matter anymore, does it?

Let me tell you the truth about what happened three years ago. My cousin and I did indeed roam along that path in the mountains and we did find a banyan forest with a cave hidden in the tree roots. And when we went into it, I was eventually trapped there. I was there for four months in the dark alone.

That was when I began to understand the power of the tree and how it is guided by the subconscious in ways we can't understand. For instance, if I wanted to place a door on a rock wall, first I had to make myself believe that there was already a door on the rock. Otherwise, that door wouldn't appear even if I scratched my head off.

It's impossible for a man to deceive his own subconscious mind, so there must be a way of guidance when using this power. This is very difficult. As I have explained to you before, once the guidance failed or if there was some kind of distraction, who knows what would appear before you? The possibilities were terrifying.

I worked at controlling my thoughts and guiding my subconscious but discovered that over time, whatever power had come to me had begun to diminish. I knew I would starve in the cave if I didn't find a way out. And then I realized what I had to do. I cloned myself and one of my bodies died while the other found himself outside the cave.

At the time, I didn't realize I was a clone. I myself and all my memories remained exactly the same. So when the body trapped in the cave began to call to me, saying I was his clone and that he would remove my existence from the world, I was sure that what I heard was some kind of monster. I removed some dynamite from my backpack and blew the cave to pieces, killing the real me and letting the copy of me survive.

I knew the power granted me by the bronze tree was waning so I grabbed a couple of its branches and left, hoping that having pieces of the tree in my possession would mean that my power wouldn't completely dwindle. I took the few treasures I had found with me, burying the branches for safekeeping once I reached the world outside. Then I was arrested in Xian when I tried to sell the objects I carried out with me.

I was in prison for three years and came home to find my mother's body—those weren't lies that I told you. That whole story was true. But there's something else you need to know.

The power given me by the bronze tree came with a cost. My memory has almost gone—if I don't write things down, they're gone forever. I think in a couple more years, I'll have no memory left at all.

You have also been given power by the tree. Maybe it will change you as it has me. I calculate that you'll retain what was given you for a few years, but your power isn't as strong as mine was, so you may not ever feel it and it may not have the same effect upon your memory. Even so, be very careful, my old friend.

Lao Yang

When I finished reading this, I found a photograph in the envelope. It was of Lao Yang and his mother on a boat in the middle of the ocean. His mother was just as I remembered her, very young, very pretty. She stood close beside her adult son, looking more like his girlfriend than his mother. I looked closely at her picture and somehow I was certain I could see a demonic ferocity on that pretty face. But after all, if I had learned nothing else from my time with the bronze tree, I at least had discovered that the mind was capable of strange tricks. What I thought I saw in the picture, I told myself, was probably only my imagination.

Coming Next:

I felt drugged by winter, so lazy that I didn't even have the energy to take a nap. Lying on my couch in a hot and stuffy room, I hovered between sleep and wakefulness, my feet like chunks of ice in spite of the hot water bottle I had placed between them. A tap on my office door snapped me out of my lethargy. "Boss, there's someone here to see you," Wang Meng, my shop assistant, announced.

"Who's crazy enough to come out on the coldest day of the year?" I grumbled as I stumbled toward the door of my shop. There was a young girl, shivering in the winter wind. "You're Lao Hai's niece," I said, grabbing her by the arm and pulling her inside. "What are you doing so far from Jinan? Wang Meng, get this poor girl some tea."

Lao Hai was a leading antique dealer and from the day I brought him Uncle Three's most precious discovery, a jade shroud from the cavern of the blood zombies, we had been business associates. His niece, Qin Haiting, was only seventeen but was already well-known among antique dealers for her knowledge and acumen. I led her into my office and made her sit on the sofa I had just vacated. I handed her my hot water bottle along with a cup of steaming tea and watched her shuddering subside.

"What brings you to this frozen city? Why did your uncle send you north at this hellish time of year?"

"He didn't want me to come, but I heard that Hangzhou

is beautiful so I ignored him. I'll know better next time. It's business that brought me here as well as curiosity. Here's a check for the fish-eye pearl you brought from the undersea tomb."

I glanced at the sum before pocketing the check; Fats would be pleased when he found out what his treasure had yielded him.

"That's not all," Qin Haiting continued, taking a letter from her handbag. "My uncle is coming to Hangzhou the day after tomorrow to go to an antique auction; he would be delighted if you would go with him. He has something he needs to talk to you about face-to-face, in private."

"The day after tomorrow?" I asked. "I don't know if I have time. Can't we talk over the phone? What could possibly be so important?"

Qin Haiting leaned close to my ear and murmured, "My uncle said he has news about a bronze fish like the ones you and your Uncle Three discovered. If you don't find time to see him, you'll always wish that you had."

TO BE CONTINUED...

Note from the Author

Back in the days when there was no television or internet and I was still a poor kid, telling stories to other children was my greatest pleasure. My friends thought my stories were a lot of fun, and I decided that someday I would become the best of storytellers.

I wrote a lot of stories trying to make that dream come true, but most of them I put away, unfinished. I completely gave up my dream of being a writer, and like many people, I sat waiting for destiny to tap me on the shoulder.

Although I gave up my dream of being a writer, luckily the dream did not give up on me. When I was 26 years old, my uncle, a merchant who sold Chinese antiques, gave me his journal that was full of short notes he had written over the years. Although fragmentary information can often be quite boring, my uncle's writing inspired me to go back to my abandoned dream. A book about a family of grave robbers began to take shape, a suspenseful novel.... I started to write again....

This is my first story, my first book that became successful beyond all expectations, a best-seller that made me rich. I have no idea how this happened, nor does anybody else; this is probably the biggest mystery of The Grave Robbers' Chronicles. Perhaps as you read the many volumes of this chronicle, you will find out why it has become so popular. I hope you enjoy the adventures you'll encounter with Uncle Three, his nephew and their companions as they roam through a world of zombies, vampires, and corpse-eaters.

Thanks to Albert Wen, Michelle Wong, Janet Brown, Kathy Mok and all my friends who helped publish the English edition of The Grave Robbers' Chronicles.

Xu Lei was born in 1982 and graduated from Renmin University of China in 2004. He has held numerous jobs, working as a graphic designer, a computer programmer, and a supplier to the U.S. gaming industry. He is now the owner of an international trading company and lives in Hangzhou, China with his wife and son. Writing isn't his day job, but it is where his heart lies.